Her Secret Fear

Zondervan Publishing House
Grand Rapids, Michigan

HER SECRET FEAR

Library of Congress Catalog Card Number 72-146566

Printed in the United States of America

Her Secret Fear

Chapter One

FROM THE WINDOW of the railway carriage, Simonette O'Shea had a grand view of the sea and the ruggedly-curved coastline. The crash of white-crested breakers mingled with the roar of the train. A cool breeze wafted through the open window, fanning her warm cheeks.

What a welcome relief from the heat of Cape Town, she reflected, a happy smile momentarily erasing her sad expression. *And what a change from Johannesburg. I never want to see Johannesburg again. Never! Oh, I do hope Mr. Stanton will consider me a suitable companion for his little daughter. I shall love it here in Sunnycove, I know.*

The train slackened pace and pulled to a halt. Her musings were rudely interrupted as a stentorian voice called: "Muizenberg Station!"

Simonette sprang to her feet. Then, sitting down again, she consulted the paper in her hand. According to the list of stations Mr. Stanton had given her over the telephone, there were still four more stations to pass before she reached her destination.

The guard blew his whistle and the train from Cape Town, hugging the jagged coastline, careered on in the direction of Simonstown.

Apart from a young couple seated in the corner, Simonette had the compartment to herself. Now the girl, meeting her companion's gaze, nodded to him, rose from her seat and sat down opposite Simonette. With a lovely smile, the girl leaned forward.

"Maybe I can help you?"

Simonette, wary of strangers, shook her head. "It's all right, thanks." Quickly she glanced at the paper in her hand. "I have to get off at Sunnycove. I see that's the station after Fish Hoek."

The girl smiled again, her eyes bright and alert in her small oval face. "Fish Hoek is where we live. I'm Leila Terblanche," she volunteered. She gestured toward her companion. "My brother Pieter. We're both schoolteachers. At present we're on holiday, but it's back to school tomorrow."

In spite of her resolve not to become friendly with anyone, Simonette's lonely heart warmed toward the girl. Leila Terblanche was small and plump, her personality as warm and radiant as her glowing red hair. Yet there was about her no restlessness, as was often the case of one who possessed a volatile temperament. There was contentment as well as joy in her expression, a deep peace which could be felt, and which spoke of a life lived close to God.

Simonette acknowledged Leila's smile, but did not deign to glance at the girl's brother. Her somber gaze flicked past the man to the scenery beyond the carriage window.

But now she did not see the sun-kissed sea, or the bright blue sky above.

* * *

Rain was pouring down; hard, rapier-like strokes were hitting the pavements of Johannesburg, deluging lawns and gardens and turning the veld into a swampland. After a dry, cold winter, the summer rains had started in earnest.

Inside the restaurant it was cozy but cool. Two electric fans silently whirred away some of the intense humidity. White-faced and strained, Simonette played nervously with the ring on her finger while she waited for her fiancé to lash out into a violent tirade.

How could she possibly marry a man of whom she was absolutely terrified? Time and time again she had endeavored to end the engagement, but each attempt had been met with storms and threats. So, for the sake of peace, she had meekly acquiesced. It wasn't as if she didn't love Robert, she argued with herself. Since the death of her parents he had become her whole world – she had lived only to please and to placate him. But now sheer desperation and the fear of becoming the wife of a "Dr. Jekyll and Mr. Hyde," had forced her to speak out. No longer could she remain silent.

Robert's hand jerked out to grip hers across the table. His eyes glittered dangerously. His handsome face, distorted by rage and passion, was almost beyond recognition.

She struggled to free her hand, but the vice-like grip tightened. She recalled the first time he had done this same thing.

Then she'd been merely puzzled and disappointed by his strange behavior. Now she was shivering with fright and had to bite her lip hard to prevent herself from crying out in terror.

* * *

Simonette felt a hand on her shoulder — the soothing, sympathetic hand of Leila Terblanche.

"My dear, you're trembling. Is anything the matter?"

The calm tones brought Simonette back to the present. She summoned a smile. "I'm all right — "

The train jolted to a standstill. Simultaneously brother and sister jumped to their feet. Leila Terblanche thrust a slip of paper into Simonette's hand.

"Here's my address and telephone number, should you wish to contact me. And here, perhaps you may care to read this." And with a farewell smile, Leila preceded her brother through the carriage doorway. Pieter nodded briefly to Simonette, but she was already thumbing through the tract Leila had handed to her.

"Christ has the solution to your problem."

A wave of annoyance washed over Simonette. So that was the motive behind Leila's kindness! She was one of those Christian women who went about trying to convert others to her way of thinking.

Deliberately Simonette tore the tract in pieces and flung them out the carriage window. A devout Catholic just did not read Protestant literature. Her priest would have a good deal to say about the matter if she did!

* * *

"That girl needs help," Leila observed, a frown creasing her serene forehead. "I'm quite convinced of it."

Pieter made no comment. Then he asked, "Did she give you her name?"

Leila shook her head regretfully. "I was about to ask her when she went into a sort of trance."

"So I noticed. She looked right past me— "

"She was shivering, poor girl. She seemed to be reliving some tragic incident." Leila paused. "I'd say she's been hurt by some man. She appeared too scared even to glance at you."

"I should say she was! But it's none of our business, Leila, so leave well enough alone."

His sister smiled. "I can do nothing else, can I? I've no idea who she is or where she lives."

"She was on her way to Sunnycove. . . ."

"That's true. But it's obvious she doesn't live there. She wasn't quite sure where to get off. That could mean she's on her way to visit someone there."

Pieter shrugged. "Maybe . . . but as I've said, it's none of our business, Leila."

"It is my business to help people. That's what I'm here for." And reprovingly she glanced up at her brother.

He smiled fondly. "All the same, your passion for helping people could land you in trouble some day."

Pieter Terblanche was shy and sensitive, his nature in many respects unlike his sparkling, extrovert sister. Yet despite their different temperaments, there existed a strong bond between them.

By now they had reached home. The house was pleasantly cool. Leila opened the venetian blinds to let in the afternoon sunshine.

"Tomorrow it's Tuesday and back to school. The summer vacation always seems to pass so quickly, even though this year we decided not to go away."

Leila was a kindergarten teacher in the local primary school, while Pieter, with his M.A. degree, taught in a suburban high school.

He followed his sister into the kitchen. She switched on the electric stove. "I daresay you're thirsty. I know I could do with a cup of tea."

Apart from a morning helper, Leila kept house for her younger brother and widowed father, who was a bank manager in Cape Town.

Pieter seated himself on a kitchen chair near the window and gazed unseeingly out onto the side garden.

"What about Dean Stanton?"

The color flew into Leila's face. She was glad her brother's gaze was focused on the red and pink geraniums that bordered the side path.

"Dean? What about him?"

Pieter swung round in his chair. "Well, last week when Dad met him on the train, Dean said he'd be phoning you about his little daughter. Remember?"

"Oh yes! He phoned last night after church. He's engaging

a companion for Wendy. Now there's no need for me to take her home from school in the afternoons. Had I known he was advertising for a companion, I'd have offered my services."

"You wouldn't!"

Leila considered a moment, her green eyes unusually thoughtful.

"You're right! I wouldn't. I'd never leave you and Dad. Besides, I gather it's a full-time job – sleep in and all that. I'd have to curtail my own activities at the church and school. I wouldn't like to do that. Besides. . . ." A frown marred Leila's smooth skin. "Dean's not too easy to get along with anymore."

"I agree there. The way he treats that daughter of his. . . ."

"I know," and Leila nodded in sympathetic agreement. "Poor little Wendy! It wasn't her fault that her mother died in giving her birth. Sharlene was always a delicate child. Even at school she was not allowed to partake in sports of any kind, I remember. Then when she married Dean, the doctor advised them to wait a few years before having a child. But Sharlene was impatient, so Dean gave in," Leila explained to her brother, who, at the time of Sharlene's death, had been an eighteen-year-old university student.

"Dean lost his wife and I lost my best friend," Leila continued. "But the worst part was his losing his faith and trust in God."

Pieter's blue eyes were pensive. "If only he'd come to church again. I know Dad has done his utmost to persuade him to attend a service. So have I and several others, but all to no avail. Dean simply refuses to darken a church doorway, not even for a wedding – or a funeral, for that matter."

"He did attend old Mr. Birch's funeral," Leila put in defensively.

"But the service was held in the funeral parlor," Pieter reminded his sister. "I daresay Dean felt he had to put in an appearance since Mr. B. was an old client of his. As the family lawyer it was Dean's duty to be present."

"Oh, well." Leila shrugged and poured out the tea. "At least he has now given his permission for Wendy to attend Sunday school."

"He has? That's great! The Lord is certainly answering prayer."

Leila nodded happily.

"Wonder what made him change his mind?" her brother inquired.

"I wouldn't know. But I'm relieved and grateful that he's no longer opposed to his daughter attending Sunday school. Wendy's seven now and no longer a baby. She has a mind of her own, that child. In looks she may resemble her mother, but in character she is so much like her father in many ways." Leila paused and helped herself to a jam tart. "Piet, wouldn't it be simply wonderful if the companion happened to be a Christian?"

"Hm. . . . It would."

Abruptly Leila changed the subject of conversation by asking: "What do you think of her – the girl we met on the train, I mean?"

"Well. . ." Pieter sipped his tea reflectively, "to tell the truth, Leila, I was a little afraid to glance at her. Somehow I gained the impression that she was going through a bad time, emotionally, I mean."

"Hm. . . . You've hit the nail on the head! That's my impression too. Perhaps she's secretly grieving. She appeared quite well-dressed and could be beautiful if she didn't look quite so forlorn and sad. Maybe she's just recently lost a loved one. It couldn't be a husband – she wore no rings on her fingers."

"Hold on, Leila!" Her brother smiled tolerantly. "It's no use conjecturing any further. You're not likely to meet her again."

"Don't be too sure! I've a strong feeling that we'll be seeing her again some day. Meanwhile, we must remember her in prayer, Piet. She seemed very much in need of prayer."

Chapter Two

A MINUTE OR TWO LATER, or so it seemed to Simonette, the train reached Sunnycove station. She almost missed the small siding set among rocks and partly hidden from the road. Somewhat bewildered by her strange surroundings, she mounted the steps leading to the exit. The crash of breakers clearly reached her ears. A thrill of anticipation shot through her. How delightfully different the Cape was from Johannesburg!

A large gray sedan was parked outside the station entrance. Mr. Stanton had told her on the telephone that he would be meeting her himself. The last time he had advertised for a companion, he had interviewed the applicant in his city office, but when the lady arrived at his Sunnycove home and saw the surroundings, she politely informed Mr. Stanton that she could not possibly consider the position. The loneliness, the isolation of the place, as well as the distance from Cape Town would drive her to distraction.

This time to avoid any confusion, he decided to interview the applicant at his home and had taken the afternoon off work especially for this purpose. As he had explained earlier to Simonette on the telephone, if she were out for a gay time, then she must look elsewhere for a post. Sunnycove was lovely in the summer. Fish Hoek beach was just around the corner and she would have plenty of opportunties to accompany his little daughter to the beach. But in the wintertime it could be pretty dreary, and the long, lonely evenings would be depressing for anyone who loved the gay lights of Town.

Simonette, however, had solemnly assured Mr. Stanton that nothing would please her better than to stay in a quiet suburb far from the city. The more isolated the place, she had mentally added, the least likely she would be to run into someone who knew her or who would perhaps recognize her. She wanted desperately to forget the past with its terror, shame and suffering. A new future stretched before her – a future she meant to grasp firmly with both hands.

If only Mr. Stanton would consider her a suitable companion!

But when she saw Dean Stanton her hopes were cruelly dashed. Her first impression of him was one of hardness – a hardness bordering on ruthlessness.

Sighting Simonette, he immediately alighted from his car, a sharp-featured, slightly-built man in his early thirties. His hawk-like eyes, as they peered into hers, were critical and unfriendly. A chill struck her heart. She was tempted to turn away and catch the next train back to Cape Town.

But then he spoke and once again the quality of his voice struck her, as it had done when he first spoke to her over the telephone. His was not the cold, clipped impersonal tone of a lawyer. His voice was strong and vibrant. Now she detected a cordial note, as if he were pleased with what he saw. But his eyes told her nothing.

Unsmiling, he opened the car door. She slid into the seat with a natural grace of movement. She was dressed in a summer suit and made an attractive picture with her smooth, shiny raven hair and fair skin. Her features were beautifully molded, her eyes large and dark gray in color.

For a fleeting moment, while he greeted her, Simonette's wistful expression had touched Dean. But he was too much of a lawyer to allow himself to be swayed or influenced in any way, particularly emotionally, when it came to the choice of a companion for his seven-year-old daughter. Sentiment had no place in his life, and would never have again, so he had vowed to himself seven long years ago.

Expertly he swung the car around and drove along the main road, returning the way he had come. Then, swinging sharply to the left and driving up the steep mountainside, he explained to Simonette that there were steps, too numerous to count, leading from the main road up to his home, but unless one was fairly agile and free from any heart complaint, it was better to walk the long way around.

"My little daughter loves to run up and down the steps, but she has been warned."

Abruptly he stopped speaking; an undecipherable expression crossed his face.

Smoothly he brought the car to a standstill in the driveway of a large, elegantly styled house.

The next instant, Simonette, sensitive to natural beauty, gave an involuntary gasp of sheer delight and surprise, as her wondering eyes took in the panorama which the house commanded.

Dean's quick, unexpected smile gave his face an elusive charm.

"You appear to find our view attractive, Miss O'Shea?"

"Attractive!" She was still feasting her gaze on the long mountain range which followed the curved coastline. "It's absolutely surpassing. I've seen pictures of the Cape, but never dreamed of anything quite like this."

"Over there to the right – that's Simonstown, our naval base. One can also travel to Cape Point that way. Then, of course," Dean pointed to the left, "there is the route along which you've just traveled, past Muizenberg and the southern suburbs back to Cape Town. But come inside. Let's talk business."

It was all so new and strange and fascinating – the calm, scintillating Indian Ocean, green rolling hills and mountains sweeping down to meet golden beaches, waves washing gently over rocks and boulders – that Simonette was loth to leave the scene. She had almost forgotten why she was there when Mr. Stanton's voice jerked her back to reality.

Slightly dazed she followed him along the winding garden path. With grave courtesy he opened the front door and led the way through the hall into a small side room which evidently was used as a study.

The cook-general, a stout, elderly black woman, thrust her head through the partly open doorway to inquire whether the master would like some tea.

"Later, Martha. Later." Dean sounded slightly irritable. "I'll ring when I want you. And please close the door behind you."

"Very good, *baas*." The woman threw a quick, inquisitive eye at Simonette before shutting the door.

Mooi missy, she mused, padding back to the kitchen. *But de baas won't want her!*

The same thought had crossed Simonette's mind as she looked up to find Dean Stanton appraising her with a directness she found definitely disturbing.

"Tell me about yourself, Miss O'Shea," he invited, tapping his pen lightly on the open pad on his desk.

A guarded, almost haunted look filled her expressive dark gray eyes.

He studied with concentration the pad in front of him.

"Simonette O'Shea," he read aloud. "Aged twenty-three . . . a kindergarten teacher in Johannesburg for three years . . . both parents dead. . . ." Dean Stanton paused. "That is all I have here. You have your teacher's diploma, of course?"

She opened her handbag at once. "Here you are, Mr. Stanton," she said, handing the document to him.

"Hm. . . ." He perused it thoughtfully. "I must compliment you. You have excellent qualifications. Now, as to your teaching ability – "

She interrupted him. "You did not require me to teach your daughter. You said she attended the local school."

"That is correct." He nodded. "The school is in Fish Hoek. Naturally you would have to supervise her homework – not that she has much. You would be required to take her to school in the mornings, then bring her home in the afternoons."

"Here are my references, Mr. Stanton. You will note that for three years I taught in the same school."

He frowned. "A convent school. So you are a Catholic, Miss O'Shea?"

"I am." She nodded proudly. "I sincerely trust that my religion will in no wise prejudice you against me."

For a long moment he did not speak. "Have I your word that you will not attempt to convert my daughter to your faith?"

"You have my promise, Mr. Stanton," her response came solemnly. "May I ask to which church you belong?"

"To no church." His expression was remote, his tone cool and unfriendly. "Now let us get back to business. I have a cook-general. The household washing is sent weekly to the laundry. You will be required to attend to my daughter's clothes, to see that she is clean and well-dressed. In the evenings you will see that she goes to bed at a reasonable time – I'm often home late, and there are times when I'm called away to the country on business. You will have Sundays off to attend – ahem – your church, as well as a free evening once a week. I trust that these arrangements suit you and that I have made everything perfectly clear, so that there will be no misunderstanding once I have engaged you. Are you satisfied with the salary I mentioned over the telephone?"

She nodded her head. "Perfectly, Mr. Stanton."

"Good!" He smiled briefly. "By the way, what nationality are you?"

She responded to his smile. "South African. My father was Irish, my mother French. They emigrated from Ireland to the Republic soon after their marriage."

Dean Stanton was tapping the blotter on his desk. "There is something I have omitted to mention to you. This position will be for one year only. Next year my daughter will be sent to boarding school. I trust this will not make any difference to you in accepting the post."

"Not at all," she assured him, unconsciously rubbing the third finger of her left hand.

"Good." His voice suddenly took on a harsh note. "I must warn you that my daughter is horribly spoiled. She has practically been brought up by her maternal grandparents, who, unfortunately, have indulged her every wish and whim. Wendy is a headstrong child who needs firm discipline. Have I made myself clear?"

"Yes, Mr. Stanton. But in my experience I have found that strict discipline, unless it is tempered with affection, is inclined to make a willful, rebellious child even worse. A little affection and love may win where discipline has failed."

He subjected her to a long, hard stare.

"I know what is best for my child," he stated coldly, "and it is not love and affection, I can assure you. She has had enough of that from her doting grandparents. At times Wendy is almost impossible to manage. What she needs is a good dose of real old-fashioned discipline. And that, Miss O'Shea, I shall leave you to administer."

Simonette stirred in her seat. Under no circumstance would she consider being employed by this tyrant, this bully, this hard, arrogant man.

She was about to decline the position when he forestalled her by saying: "By the way, there is something I have omitted to ask you. What made you relinquish your teaching post in the Transvaal and come to the Cape? And why accept this post instead of that of a kindergarten teacher?"

Because courtesy came naturally to her, she made reply.

"It was seeing your advertisement in the paper that gave me the idea of becoming a companion. I thought it would be lovely to belong to a family." She hesitated fingering her handbag. "But as to my reason for leaving Johannesburg, surely that is a personal matter? I have no desire to discuss it."

Simonette's reaction surprised Dean Stanton. The girl had spirit after all. He smiled, the amusement in his eyes not quite erasing the bitterness and hardness.

"I shall respect your wishes, Miss O'Shea. As you say, it is your own affair." He paused. "Now, when is the earliest you can commence?"

She had risen to her feet, fully intending to tell Mr. Stanton that she had changed her mind, that she was sorry she could not accept his offer.

But the opening door and a child's accusing cry, cut short her words.

"Daddy! Why didn't you tell me!"

"Wendy!" her father chided coldly. "Please leave the room at once! How many times have I told you not to disturb me when I'm busy?"

But the small girl took not the slightest notice of her father's reprimand. Her gaze was riveted on Simonette, her large baby blue eyes shining with unconcealed admiration.

"You're beautiful and you look kind." Wendy turned appealingly to her father. "Daddy, I think I'd like this lady to look after me. Please say yes!" Then, without waiting for an answer, she took Simonette's hand. "You will, won't you?"

Simonette wrestled with her thoughts. She perceived the almost desperate appeal in the child's blue eyes. It was fairly obvious that Wendy Stanton was in great need of love and understanding. She was a pretty girl – the prettiest little girl Simonette had ever seen – yet there was about her a pathetic air that went straight to the older girl's sympathetic heart.

"Please, Miss – " the child was clutching her hand frantically.

"Wendy!" her father exclaimed in a cold, commanding voice. "Can't you see you're embarrassing Miss O'Shea?"

Impulsively Simonette put an arm round the slim shoulders and fondled the child's golden curls. Shyly, as if unused to affectionate demonstrations, Wendy gazed up at Simonette, an expression of utter trust and devotion on her face.

Involuntarily Simonette experienced a constricted feeling in her throat. The child trusted her – Simonette would not fail her. She could not refuse now – the child needed her – needed her guidance and affection. . . .

Simonette sighed inwardly. If only she herself had someone in whom she could put her trust!

Chapter Three

DEAN STANTON SEEMED in a happier, more contented frame of mind when he entered the offices of de Klerk, Stanton & Co. the next morning.

So thought his secretary, Olivia de Klerk, who for many years had been sensitive to his every mood. A tall, strongly-built woman of thirty, with dark, restless eyes and a passionate mouth, she had been in love with her employer since the age of twenty-one. Dean Stanton had just been appointed junior partner at the time Olivia had entered her uncle's firm.

She had been filled with shocked disappointment and jealousy when he had announced his engagement to Sharlene Pearson, who, in Olivia's opinion, was an insipid, weak-willed girl, hardly a fit companion for the energetic, ambitious Dean. He could well afford to wait until he was properly established before rushing headlong into marriage with an unsuitable partner, Olivia had told him quite bluntly.

But Dean, young, eager and desperately in love, had merely given his secretary a helpless shrug.

What fools, Olivia had reflected in disgust, men were when it came to choosing a wife!

After the marriage, Sharlene would occasionally call in at the office to see her husband. And how Olivia would despise the fragile, fairy-like girl with the corn-colored hair and innocently smiling lips. However, Olivia was swift to detect the expession of fear which lurked in the younger girl's large blue eyes. Sharlene Stanton was terrified of having a child!

"It was fear that killed Sharlene," Olivia intimated to those who were curious enough to discuss the tragic incident with her. "Poor Dean! So young to be left with a motherless child."

A pity, Olivia mused, lifting up a pile of correspondence

from her desk, that Dean had decided to engage a companion for his daughter. Why couldn't he have let the child remain with her grandparents? It had been an ideal arrangement that Mr. and Mrs. Pearson should care for their granddaughter.

Well, Olivia shrugged philosophically, Dean was not likely to choose some young, glamorous girl as his daughter's companion. A middle-aged, severe-looking widow was sure to be his choice – or maybe some plump, jolly kindergarten teacher like Leila Terblanche, who instinctively seemed to know how to handle the young.

Feeling somewhat reassured, Olivia advanced into her chief's office, a smile curving her full red lips.

At her entry, Dean glanced up from some papers on his desk. He acknowledged her smile.

"I think at last I've managed to find the right sort of companion for Wendy. Let's hope so! She's starting tomorrow. I'm fetching her this evening after work and driving her out to Sunnycove. At present she is staying in a Cape Town hotel."

"Who is she, Dean? Anyone I know?"

He shook his head. "She's from Johannesburg. Never been to the Cape before now. She seems a fairly pleasant type – quiet and reserved. A little sad-looking, though. . . . Wendy took to her at once, I'm glad to say."

Quiet and reserved. . . . Hastily Olivia veiled her relief. A middle-aged companion, no doubt.

"That's nice to know," Olivia murmured.

"Yes," continued Dean, evidently in one of his communicative moods. "She's only twenty-three – "

"Only twenty-three!" echoed Olivia, too stunned to school her expression.

Dean smiled at her obvious dismay. "I wouldn't let that worry you, Olivia. Miss O'Shea looks older than her years. A responsible sort, I'd say. It's my belief she came down here to get over some broken romance. During our interview she kept feeling for the ring that is no longer on her finger."

"Miss O'Shea. . . . So that's her name. Is she pretty, Dean?"

"Trust a woman to ask that!" He laughed in mock amusement. "Yes, Simonette O'Shea is pretty. But that is hardly an apt word to describe her. Beautiful is more fitting. Not strikingly beautiful – but lovely in a gentle, refined sort of way. One has to look at her twice before realizing her beauty."

Oh dear! groaned Olivia inwardly, her hopes of becoming

the second Mrs. Stanton fast disappearing from view. Perhaps she was a fool to keep on turning down offers of marriage for the sake of Dean Stanton.

"You're wasting your time, my girl," her bachelor uncle would frequently declare. "Dean will never marry again. He's the type who will remain true to the memory of one woman. He was very devoted to Sharlene, remember!"

While Dean is still free, I guess I'll just go on hoping, Olivia told herself, feeding the paper into her typewriter.

Simonette had not expected Dean Stanton to bring his secretary with him when he called for her after office hours at the hotel.

"Let me come with you to meet Miss O'Shea," Olivia had begged him. "I'd like to be friends with her."

Dean agreed it was a good idea and suggested that Olivia might even care to drive down with them to Sunnycove and stay to dinner.

She was more than delighted with the prospect, for she knew that afterwards he would feel obliged to drive her back to Town.

During lunch hour she went home to change into a smart green dress which set off her dark hair and olive complexion.

After the introduction, the two girls covertly studied each other. Simonette's soft blue ensemble lent her a fragile air which made her even more ethereal in her beauty. Her sad, smoky gray eyes glowed with a gentle light; a delicate pink tinged her smooth white cheeks.

Olivia experienced a swift, sharp stab of jealousy. But she was too much of a dissembler to reveal her feelings, especially in the presence of Dean. So she smiled graciously at the younger girl.

But Simonette was not so easily deceived. Whereas she had taken an instant liking to the frank, jolly-looking Leila Terblanche, this young woman who was Dean's secretary, with her dark, arrogant looks, deep-throated voice and almost masculine figure, filled Simonette with consternation. Olivia de Klerk was friendly enough, but the younger girl's intuition warned her to walk warily.

Olivia did most of the talking on the drive down, with Dean occasionally interrupting to point out various places of interest to Simonette, who sat in the back seat.

When they arrived at Sunnycove, old Martha came ambling

out and offered to help Simonette with the luggage. Handing the servant a suitcase, Dean told her he would manage the rest.

The long, combination living room-dining room, the large main bedroom and Wendy's room all overlooked the front garden, while the room to which Dean took Simonette's luggage, had a corner window with a view toward Simonstown. Dean's study faced the Fish Hoek side. Since his wife's death seven years ago, he had taken to sleeping on the couch in his study. Mr. and Mrs. Pearson, his parents-in-law, occupied the main bedroom whenever they came to stay. In the earlier days their visits had been fairly frequent, but these days it was usual for them to spend only one weekend a month at Sunnycove.

Absorbed with her crayons and coloring book, Wendy had not heard the arrival of her father's car. Now becoming aware of some commotion going on in the adjoining room, she scampered out into the corridor. Simonette glanced up to see the little girl standing wistfully on the threshold.

"Hullo!" Wendy's greeting was solemn. Then, ignoring her father, she came into Simonette's room.

Shyly the child caught hold of her new companion's hand. Simonette bent down and kissed Wendy lightly on the cheek.

"Wendy!" There was a look of mild reproach on her father's face. "Don't I get a greeting, too?"

"Sorry, Daddy." But his daughter did not sound in the least crestfallen nor did she raise her head for his kiss. Dean gave a nonchalant shrug of his slim shoulders, as the child turned her attention again to her new companion.

Simonette, realizing that it was not usual for father and daughter to kiss each other, immediately wondered why.

Their relationship is a strange one, Simonette mused.

"Come into the lounge when you are ready, Miss O'Shea." With these words Dean Stanton left her abruptly.

Because of his strict Christian upbringing, Dean neither smoked nor imbibed strong drink, much to Olivia's disgust. He was handing her a glass of pure apple juice when Simonette entered the lounge holding Wendy's hand. The little girl cradled a baby doll in her free arm.

At the sight of her father's secretary, Wendy gave a start of shocked disappointment. Instead of greeting Olivia, the child pulled a wry face.

"Wendy!" Sternly Dean scolded his daughter. "Where are your manners, child?"

She stared at her father a shade defiantly.

"Please say good evening to Miss de Klerk."

Olivia, seething inwardly, gave a sugary smile and invited the little girl to sit with her on the couch.

About to refuse, Wendy intercepted her father's warning glance, and not wishing to disgrace herself in her new companion's eyes, slid obediently onto the settee.

"It's back to school for Wendy," Olivia observed with simulated interest. "Do you like your lessons?"

The child was silent. She did not consider it worth her while to converse with her father's secretary. Past experience had taught her that Miss de Klerk's interest in her was not quite sincere.

Cuddling her doll close, the little girl whispered: "She doesn't really like us – she's only pretending 'cause she wants to marry daddy. But we won't let her, will we, dolly?"

Olivia's sharp ears clearly distinguished the murmured words. The impulse to slap Dean's child was fierce, demanding satisfaction.

Deliberately Olivia maneuvered the heel of her shoe to come in sharp contact with the child's slippered foot.

Engaged in conversation with Simonette, Dean scarcely heard his daughter's stifled gasp of pain, but Simonette did. Surreptitiously she'd been watching the two figures on the couch.

A minute later Olivia's furious cry filled the room. It was so loud and piercing that even the old cook hastened from her domain to inquire what was going on.

"You little vixen!" Olivia stormed angrily. "How dare you pinch me?"

"I did not!" the child answered in a tone of injured innocence. "I did not pinch you, Miss de Klerk."

"I demand an instant apology." Olivia glared at Dean, almost as if he were the culprit.

"What on earth is going on?" Frowning heavily he met his secretary's angry stare. Then sharply he addressed his little daughter. "What mischief have you been up to now?"

"Why, nothing, daddy," she replied innocently, "I've done nothing at all."

"That's not true!" Olivia's face was flushed with mortification and fury. "Your daughter had the audacity to pinch me."

"Did you, Wendy?"

"Of course she did!" Olivia exclaimed.

"I'm asking Wendy."

"I did not," she reiterated with emphasis, "pinch Miss de Klerk."

"Then what do you call it, I'd like to know." Olivia glanced across at Simonette, as if appealing to her for sympathy.

"Did you pinch Miss de Klerk, Wendy?" Simonette quietly asked the child.

Candidly Wendy returned her gaze. She solemnly shook her head.

"No, Miss O'Shea. I did not. My dolly did."

Simonette could not entirely conceal her smile. She knew enough about child psychology to realize that Wendy fully believed she was speaking the truth in blaming her doll.

"Wendy!" her father's voice vibrated with indignation. "You will apologize this instant. First, for pinching Miss de Klerk, and then for lying on top of it."

"But, Daddy, I did not! Look – I'll prove it." Firmly holding the doll's arm, Wendy was on the point of manipulating the tiny fingers into Olivia's flesh, when the latter jumped to her feet, her face crimson with wrath.

"I absolutely refuse to tolerate such behavior. Please take me home, Dean."

"There's no need to upset yourself, Olivia. I shall most certainly deal with Wendy. Such disgraceful behavior!" His eyes were hard and unyielding as he looked at his daughter. "Now apologize at once and get to your room. . . ."

"But – Daddy – "

He ignored her protests. "As punishment you will have dinner alone in your room tonight."

"But you promised!" The blue eyes spilled over with tears. "You said I could stay up this evening and have dinner with you and Miss O'Shea. Please! I apologize to Miss de Klerk for dolly's bad manners. But dolly was upset – Miss de Klerk hurt me first – "

"How dare you!"

"Please!" Dean raised a deprecating hand. "Go to your room at once, Wendy."

Clutching her doll tightly, the child rushed from the lounge. She was sobbing brokenly.

Simonette rose to her feet, feeling slightly disconcerted by the turn of events. She made for the door.

"Miss O'Shea," Dean called, following her into the hall. "I'd rather you left Wendy alone for the moment."

"But it's all so unfair!" Simonette's gray eyes held his unwilling gaze. "Mr. Stanton, your daughter firmly believes she was speaking the truth when she told you her doll pinched Miss de Klerk. Don't forget how imaginative most children are. And Wendy may have been goaded, you know."

"Are you suggesting — "

"Your daughter was definitely goaded, so don't blame her too much." Simonette hesitated. "I would not have told you this, but — "

"Well, go on." His fine brows arched inquiringly.

"In fairness to Wendy, I suggest you keep your promise. A broken promise is almost beyond pardon in a child's eyes. Guilty or not, she has done her part by apologizing to Miss de Klerk. Mr. Stanton, please do forgive your daughter."

The words, softly spoken, held an underlying note of passion. Dean regarded Simonette speculatively before giving his response.

"Very well," he said at length, "you may tell Wendy she will be allowed to dine with us this evening."

"Thank you, Mr. Stanton. I shall go and tell Wendy at once."

At this unexpected victory, Simonette's heart filled with joy. Perhaps, after all, her task would not be quite so difficult as she had at first feared.

Chapter Four

IT WAS A DELIGHTFUL morning, not too hot, just pleasantly warm as the sun was still low in the sky.

Simonette decided to walk with Wendy to school and not make use of the car her employer had placed at her disposal. Dean usually caught the eight o'clock train which arrived at Cape Town station just before nine. Because of parking problems it was only on rare occasions that he drove the car into Town during office hours.

Having left her charge safely at the school gates, Simonette took the train back to Sunnycove. She was anxious to return to the house as quickly as possible to tidy her room.

Taking the shortcut via the steps up to the house, she arrived, puffing and panting and sat down on a garden bench to recover her breath. Her brow was damp with perspiration from the unaccustomed exercise.

The next moment old Martha ambled outside, brandishing a large sunshade.

"Missy will get the sunstroke!" she cried, her eyes rolling in horror.

Smiling, Simonette accepted the sunshade, then rose to her feet and followed the cook-general indoors.

"Oh, Martha! You shouldn't have!" Simonette expostulated, though not unpleased to find her room tidied and the bed neatly made. "You have so much to do without bothering with my room. I would have done it before taking Wendy to school, only we left half an hour earlier than the arranged time. But thanks so much, Martha. It was sweet of you."

The old servant beamed with pleasure. Miss O'Shea was a real lady, she decided. Not like that stuck-up Miss de Klerk. . . .

There were some socks of Wendy's that needed darning,

two buttons were missing off her cardigan which had to be replaced, and a tear in her nightgown needed to be mended.

These, together with a work basket, Simonette carried out into the shaded side garden. A cool mountain breeze touched her warm cheeks.

How pleasant it all was, how peaceful! The sunlight scintillating on the blue waters, the gentle lapping of waves on the rocks below; the joyous twitter of birds as they called to one another from the interlacing branches of treetops.

Once more Simonette began to feel the pulse of life flowing through her. There was every hope that she would enjoy working and living at Sunnycove. This morning Dean Stanton seemed more kindly disposed toward her. For this she was grateful.

At the dinner table last night, Dean's secretary had been unsuccessful in concealing her curiosity. What had caused Simonette to come to Cape Town? And what had prompted her to relinquish her teaching career? Why accept a post as child's companion instead?

Simonette, constantly on guard, had deftly evaded answering questions which were motivated, not by genuine interest, but by sheer inquisitiveness.

"And what of your young man?" Olivia interrogated archly, sipping coffee and flinging Simonette a quick, suggestive glance.

Standing with his back to the lounge window and surveying the two girls with some amusement, Dean suddenly sensed Simonette's inner confusion. Gallantly he came to her rescue. Although her hedging answers puzzled him, he would not allow Olivia to pester the younger girl with her pertinent and awkward questions.

"That's enough, Olivia." The finality in his tone brooked no further argument. "It's time to go, anyway."

Simonette gave him a smile in which both relief and gratitude were blended.

Unexpectedly he found himself returning her smile.

With a disdainful shrug Olivia set down her cup on the coffee table and followed Dean into the hall.

At first both were somewhat reticent on the journey back to Cape Town. Then, as the car nosed its way up the steep incline leading to Olivia's Oranjezicht flat, she could no longer contain her suspicious thoughts.

"In my opinion there's something dubious about that girl you've taken on as Wendy's companion."

"Can't say I exactly care for your insinuations, Olivia." His brow was creased in displeasure. He would not easily forget the distasteful scene his secretary had created earlier in the evening. Secretly he admired the manner in which Simonette had handled an embarrassing situation. But for her intervention, the rift between himself and his daughter would have been widened still further.

In spite of himself, Wendy's surprising good night kiss had touched him deeply.

"Thank you for letting me stay up to dinner, daddy," she had whispered childishly in his ear.

Olivia's deep voice intruded. "I'm not insinuating anything. I'm stating a fact, Dean. A kindergarten teacher condescending to be a child's companion. . . ."

He stifled a yawn. "There's nothing unusual about that. Miss O'Shea wanted a change from teaching. Besides, she'll be supervising Wendy's homework – "

"But the pay!" Olivia's voice rose. "How is she going to manage on a smaller salary unless she has private means?"

"That's Miss O'Shea's worry," Dean's response was dry. "It's no concern of yours, Olivia. Please remember that."

"What exactly are you paying her?" Olivia was unable to repress her query.

"The same salary as she'd normally receive as a teacher in a primary school. Hope you're satisfied." He spoke shortly.

"Oh." Dean's secretary was taken aback.

His car slid to a standstill outside a fashionable block of flats.

"But what of Miss O'Shea's board and lodging?" Olivia ventured to ask. "Surely you're charging her something for that?"

"It's no concern of yours, Olivia," Dean reiterated with some irritation. "Goodnight. See you at work tomorrow."

"But aren't you coming in?"

He arched an eyebrow. "Do I usually?"

No, he did not. It was usual for him to plead an excuse.

His sarcasm annoyed her, but she managed to check her feelings and hold out a placating hand.

"Dean. . . . Sorry if I've offended you this evening. Won't you come indoors just for a few moments? It's still early. Please!"

"I'm tired, Olivia."

"You tired?" She gazed at him with some surprise.

Dean, the indefatigable, the high pressure worker, the slave driver, as some of the office staff called him.

He smiled wearily. "So if you don't mind, Olivia. . . ."

"Of course not. But it's so unlike you to feel tired."

"The years are catching up on me, I'm afraid."

"But you're still young. Just two years older than I," Olivia protested.

I'm the one who is getting old, Olivia groaned inwardly. *Dean isn't. Not really. Apart from his expression which has grown hard and a trifle cynical, his physical appearance hasn't changed much since the day he'd married Sharlene eight years ago. He is still lean and slight of build. Too thin, really,* Olivia mused. *He should be putting on a little weight. If Sharlene had lived, he would no doubt have settled down to being a happy husband and father. Now he is a highly successful lawyer. But he is far from happy.*

She made no move to get out of the car.

"Dean, before you go, I'd like to speak to you. It's about Miss O'Shea."

He sighed audibly. "I think we've discussed her enough, don't you?"

"I've an odd feeling about that girl, Dean."

"Oh, skip it!"

Olivia ignored the rebuke. "I've an idea she's running away from someone or something. Perhaps there's a husband in the background."

"She's not married – "

"Maybe she's a divorcee – " Olivia suggested.

"Definitely not! Besides, Miss O'Shea is a Roman Catholic."

"A Catholic!" echoed Olivia with raised eyebrows. "You don't say! Aren't you afraid she might influence Wendy?"

"Not at all. Miss O'Shea has my instructions. She is not at all likely to disobey them." He hesitated. "Better a Roman Catholic than no faith at all. Like you, Olivia."

"What about yourself, Dean?" she flung accusingly at him.

"At least I used to be a church-goer." He heaved a deep sigh. "I was happy in those days. In a way I wish – " Suddenly he halted. "I've agreed to allow Leila Terblanche to take Wendy to Sunday school."

It's a beginning, anyway. . . . Dean paused in his reflections. *Maybe one day I'll be persuaded to return to church. But*

I made a vow. . . . When God took Sharlene, I vowed I wouldn't attend a place of worship again. . . .

Did God take pleasure in breaking hearts – in leaving a newborn baby motherless? Through the years that followed his wife's death, these bitter questions would erupt to the surface of his mind to torture and torment him again and again.

Olivia's voice cut short his cogitations.

"Now Wendy will be torn between the two – Leila's faith on the one hand and the new companion's Roman Catholic doctrine. Wendy will have to make a choice."

"There can be no question of a choice." Dean spoke with some asperity. "On Sundays Leila will fetch Wendy. Miss O'Shea, I presume, will attend her own church. I shall not require her services on Sundays, so she'll be free to attend mass or confession – or whatever they may have at her church. . . ."

Simonette's thoughts were running along similar lines as she sat sewing in the side garden. She was glad her employer had said she could have Sundays off. As a staunch Catholic it was her duty to attend mass on as many mornings as possible, but especially on Sundays.

This morning on her way back from taking Wendy to the Fish Hoek school, Simonette had spotted a little Catholic church near the station. She must remember to look up the train time table just in case it rained on Sunday and she'd be unable to walk to church.

In her heart Simonette was not looking forward to attending the services as much as she'd done in her younger days. She was duty bound to attend the confessional, and that meant raking up the past – the past she was doing her utmost to bury.

Suddenly, her dark gray eyes clouded with distress and anxiety, as unhappy recollections enveloped her. She was blind to everything save incidents of the past.

Her late fiancé's uncle was a priest, and Simonette and Robert had attended the church together where he officiated.

With startling clarity she recalled the last time she had visited the confessional. It had been prior to her leaving Johannesburg for Cape Town.

"It is good, my child, that you have taken steps to start a new life for yourself." Clearly she heard again the priest's calm voice. "But it is a great pity that you have decided against taking holy vows. In the convent you would find forgetfulness. . . ."

But, father, I have no desire to become a nun, Simonette

had cried inwardly. Surely there must be some other way in which she could find forgetfulness and peace of mind?

"Ponder it, my child. We are all required to make retribution for our sins. Remember you have been guilty in sending an innocent man to his death – a man who had before him a great future – a man you were pledged to marry. Because of your willful refusal to go through with the ceremony, you caused his untimely death."

Sick with sorrow and despair, Simonette tried in vain to shut out the priest's voice.

"In the convent you can work out your own salvation." Inexorably her father confessor went on. "In the cloistered life you will find peace and solace for your heart. Think it over, my child. Think it over well."

"But I have, father! I have!" Her gentle voice rose slightly. "I do not feel called to be a nun. I am still young, father. I want to live – "

Sternly he had interpolated: "You want to live while your fiancé lies cold in his grave. Shame on you! My child, you are being selfish – utterly selfish. . . ."

Softly Simonette began to weep. The sobs she had choked back could be stifled no longer. The tears flowed freely.

The priest let her cry. Then, when she had regained her composure, he spoke again.

"Now don't forget, when you are settled," he exhorted, "to let me know the name of your new father confessor, so that I can send him your case history. . . ."

So, sighed Simonette, what was the use of trying to forget? As soon as she made herself known to the priest in the parish, he would be calling on her, no doubt, to offer suggestions as to how she could best make expiation for her sins. And the inevitable nunnery solution would again crop up.

Perhaps that's where God wants me after all. Simonette frowned against the strong sunlight peeping through the foliage of the tree under which she sat.

"Here's a cuppa tea, Missy."

Beaming broadly, the old servant, carrying a tray, waddled toward Simonette.

"Oh Martha!" Simonette protested playfully, catching sight of the freshly baked scones. "At this rate you'll be spoiling me dreadfully."

Glancing down at her watch, she saw it was later than she'd

expected. Soon it would be time for her to fetch Wendy from school.

The noon sun was hot and burning, so Simonette took the short cut via the steps to the station. She was just in time to catch the train, and arrived at the school after the bell had sounded.

She took up her position at the school gates to wait for her little charge. After standing for over five minutes Simonette began to wonder whether she'd somehow missed Wendy. Perhaps she had been among the first pupils to come out of school. Simonette knew a moment of panic.

Then the next instant she breathed in relief. The child was hopping gaily across the playground, but she was not alone. In one hand she clutched her little suitcase, but her other hand was held by a young woman. One of the teachers, no doubt.

As they drew nearer, Simonette gave a start of recognition. The young woman holding Wendy's hand was Leila Terblanche!

Chapter Five

WENDY DROPPED LEILA'S hand to clutch Simonette's possessively.

"So you're Miss O'Shea." Leila was smiling at Simonette and thinking how astonished her brother would be to learn that Wendy's new companion was none other than the sad-looking girl they had met on the train.

"Wendy has told me so much about you," Leila went on, with a genuine attempt at friendliness. "She insisted that I come with her to meet you. I'm glad now that I did."

"So am I," rejoined Simonette, her poised dignity slipping from her like a cloak.

Leila Terblanche, sincere and warm-hearted, was so different from Olivia de Klerk. After last night's unpleasant incident, it was a welcome relief to meet someone with whom she could perhaps strike up some sort of friendship. And like herself, Leila Terblanche was a schoolteacher. There was mutual interest. Of course, their faiths differed widely. But then, Simonette argued with herself, it should be fairly easy to steer clear of the subject of religion.

"You and Wendy must come to tea one afternoon," Leila suggested. "How about tomorrow?"

"Please say yes, Miss O'Shea!" Wendy's grip on her hand tightened.

"Well – I should really ask Mr. Stanton if it's all right."

"'Course it will be all right," Wendy hastened to assure Simonette. "Aunty Leila and daddy are old friends."

"All the same I shall ask your father, Wendy." Simonette turned to the older girl. "Thanks for the invitation, Miss Terblanche."

"Please call me Leila."

"I'd like to." Simonette smiled a little shyly. "And my name is Simonette."

"What a pretty name. Well – 'bye for now. See you both tomorrow. Wendy will show you the way, Simonette." And with a wave of her hand, Leila hurried back to the school building.

"Guess who I met today," Leila remarked to her brother at tea time. "Simonette O'Shea."

He wrinkled his brow. "Never heard of her. Who is she?"

"Wendy's new companion. I've invited them both over to tea tomorrow afternoon."

"Now I know what you made these for." Pieter smiled as he sampled another of the batch of small cakes his sister had just baked. "These taste jolly good."

Leila smiled mischievously. "You'll never guess who she is."

"Who?" Pieter asked absently.

"The new companion, of course!" Leila's eyes were dancing merrily.

"Miss O'Shea. . . ." He was munching heartily. "Can't say I've heard of her. What's she like?"

"You've seen her. She's the girl we met Monday afternoon on the train."

"You don't say!" Pieter sounded surprised.

"I knew that would shake you." His sister smiled at him. "I was right. I had a queer feeling we'd meet again some day, but didn't think it would be so soon. She's a lovely person, Piet, really beautiful. If only she didn't look quite so dejected – "

"Is she a Christian?"

Regretfully Leila shook her head. "From what I gathered from Wendy, I don't think she is a real Christian, but she is a member of the Roman Catholic church."

"Then I'm surprised that Dean employed her," Pieter murmured reflectively.

"I'm not – "

"But Dean's not a man to be influenced by a woman's looks," Pieter declared.

"I know that!" *All the same,* Leila mused, *Dean married Sharlene – not me . . . and Sharlene was pretty – very pretty.*

Deftly Leila gathered up the tea things and carried the tray through to the kitchen.

"Now I must get on with supper. Dad has a meeting right afterwards and wants to eat early." She paused and looked earnestly at her brother. "Hope you'll be home early from school tomorrow. I'd like you to meet Simonette O'Shea."

"I'll do my best," promised Pieter. "Yes, I'd like to meet her again. Quite frankly, Leila, Miss O'Shea interests me a great deal. As you say, there is something about her. Call it an air of mystery, if you like."

Leila nodded. She pondered a moment. "I suspect that her depression and unhappiness stem from unresolved problems."

"Yes . . . you could be right, Leila. I want to help the girl, too." There was a strange expression on her brother's face.

Pieter Terblanche was attractive in a rugged, masculine sort of way. Of sturdy build, he had sandy hair, a sprinkling of freckles, gentle blue eyes and a shy smile. His composure and reserve successfully hid the fact that he was a strict disciplinarian which many an errant pupil had discovered to his cost. The young geometry master did not easily become angry or ruffled. By his steady Christian witness he had led many a rebellious teenager to the Lord. Besides being very religious, as his pupils termed Pieter, he was also a keen sportsman, an excellent swimmer, and played a really smashing game of cricket. All this the schoolboys could admire and respect.

As it was the commencement of the school year and the sports program for the term had not yet been drawn up, Pieter was able to be home in time to meet Simonette.

They were having tea on the veranda as he pulled the family car to a standstill in the gravel driveway. Leila had insisted that her brother make use of the car, so that he could also join in the little tea party.

"Wendy would hate to miss her Uncle Pieter. And you said yourself that you'd like to meet Simonette O'Shea," Leila had added quickly, knowing his reluctance to attend tea parties.

"My brother is also a school teacher," Leila explained to Simonette later, when Pieter had arrived. "Pieter is a high school master in the suburbs."

Simonette held out her hand in greeting. He clasped hers warmly.

Simonette took an immediate liking to Pieter just as she had done to his sister. There was something so solid and worthwhile about him. When she first saw him on the train, she was too grief-stricken to observe him fully. But now she could see what a fine, steady young man he was.

"What a lovely garden you have," she gestured toward the

trim, green lawns and gay flower beds. "Do you care for gardening?" Simonette smiled at Pieter. There was, despite the warmth of her smile, a hint of reserve in her manner.

"I haven't much time, really. What with sports, correcting homework, attending meetings and church, my days are fully occupied." Pieter sat down on a vacant chair, while his sister poured the tea.

"We have a weekly garden boy," Leila put in, "but I do most of the planting. Whenever I have a spare moment you'll find me out and about in the garden. But it makes me no slimmer," she added with a gay little laugh. "Guess I'll always be the plump and comfortable kind. I'm not one for dieting, I love my food too much for that. I have a hearty appetite – and not a day's illness in my life, thank God."

"You certainly look the picture of health," Simonette murmured, glancing appreciatively at the older girl's glowing cheeks. "No matter what I eat or do I simply can't put on weight."

"You'll always be the lean kind, I reckon," Leila replied. Like Dean, Leila added mentally. All the same, Simonette was totally unlike Dean in nature. There was no comparison, really. Yet this girl had also suffered, was still suffering, of that Leila was sure. Even her gentle smile could not erase the hurt that lurked in her eyes.

"So you were also a kindergarten teacher." Pieter looked earnestly across the table at Simonette. "In which part of Johannesburg was that?"

She hesitated a moment. "Rosebank," she rejoined briefly. Another lengthy pause, then, "I taught there for three years – my first post after I qualified."

"Did you enjoy living in Johannesburg?" Leila asked.

Simonette nodded. "But not as much as I'm going to enjoy staying in the Cape."

"Any relatives?"

The younger girl shook her head. "My parents died just before I started teaching. It was rather lonely living on my own, so I sold everything and went to stay in a hotel. Unfortunately I'm an only child," Simonette added with a smile.

"Sorry about your parents, Simonette." Leila's voice was filled with compassion.

There were so many questions Pieter longed to ask, but prudence kept him from voicing them.

However, Leila failed to control her curiosity. "Was that why you decided to come down to the Cape?"

It was rather a tactless question, Pieter reflected, since Simonette had just remarked that she lost her parents over three years ago – prior to her taking a teaching post.

Though she was perfectly composed, he caught the confusion in her smoky gray eyes.

Pieter stood up. Discreetly he changed the subject. "Leila, I think I'll take Prince for a short run."

At the mention of his name, the large collie dog sleeping at Pieter's feet, began to raise himself lazily to a sitting position.

"Oh, please let me come too!" Wendy, who had been quietly playing on the lawn, was instantly at Pieter's side. "I'm not a bit afraid of Prince. See." Gingerly the child touched the dog's shaggy ear.

Pieter smiled fondly. "I know you're not. All right, you may come, Wendy. See you again before you leave, Simonette."

"Prince is too powerful for me," Leila observed to Simonette. "I never take him for a walk – I leave that to Dad and Pieter. In the morning he's kept locked up in the back garden. More tea, Simonette?"

She shook her head. "No thanks. It was a lovely tea. Hope your brother won't be too long. We should be making our way back to Sunnycove."

"You're not to worry. Pieter will run you back with pleasure."

"Don't you drive?"

Leila grimaced. "Only when absolutely necessary. I have a license, but seldom make use of the car, except on Sundays when I fetch some of the pupils to Sunday school. At last Dean has allowed Wendy to attend. It was a terrific job to persuade him, I can tell you."

"He's against religion then? When he employed me he made me promise not to try to influence his daughter."

Leila had suspected as much, but she did not voice her thoughts.

Guardedly she rejoined, "I wouldn't say he's against religion. Wendy's mother died in giving her birth. It was a real tragedy. It fairly broke Dean's heart. He's not been the same since Sharlene passed away. She and Dean were both members of our church. Sharlene was a sweet little Christian, though somewhat nervous and timid." Leila paused. "Now Dean is a backslider, I'm sorry to say." Her green eyes held deep regret. "But we're all praying earnestly that he'll come back to the Lord."

It was almost with a sense of wonder that Simonette listened to the older girl speaking. There was something so confident, so personal in the way she said the Lord's name. Leila spoke as if He were a friend, someone she knew quite intimately.

Never before had Simonette met anyone quite like Leila Terblanche. If only she herself had someone other than the priest in whom she could confide. She did not relish the thought of attending the confessional on Saturday, which was the day confessions were heard, according to the notice board outside the Roman Catholic church. She would then have to make herself known to the priest and once again the long recitation of her past sins would begin.

Simonette gave a helpless shrug. So what was the use of starting a new life? Perhaps if she agreed to enter the convent, as her father confessor in Johannesburg had suggested, she would find peace of mind and heart. But surely there must be some other way out? She did not feel called to be a nun. . . .

But had she committed such a dreadful crime after all? How could she possibly have married a "Dr. Jekyll and Mr. Hyde" personality?

In vain she tried to obliterate Robert's image from her mind. She saw him again as she first knew him – good-looking, gay, and with a charm that had captivated her from the start. She had loved him so desperately, almost as desperately as he had loved her.

They had met at a teachers' meeting. Like Pieter Terblanche, Robert was also a high school teacher. But unlike Pieter, Robert was much older than Simonette – thirty-five years to her twenty-one. He was a gifted and brilliant teacher, but also intense and high-strung. A neurotic! This she had discovered later to her loss.

Everyone agreed he had a great future ahead of him. He had applied for a headship and was positive his application would be accepted. And it was. . . .

Their engagement to be married coincided with his being appointed head of the high school which adjoined the primary school where Simonette taught. Her happiness was complete and her future assured. Nothing could possibly go wrong now.

But it did!

They planned to marry early in the new year, so that they

could make use of the long summer vacation. Simonette would continue with her teaching for about a year.

Blissfully she began to collect her trousseau, hardly aware that some of her colleagues secretly envied her. As an only child she was diffident about making friends and kept herself a little aloof from the rest of the staff.

However, after her engagement to the handsome headmaster, Simonette opened like a flower to the sun. Love animated her somber gray eyes; she shed her reserve like a cloak and had a friendly smile for everyone.

It was wonderful to be in love! No one could have been happier than she and Robert.

But gradually, almost imperceptibly at first, things began to change. Not their affection for each other, that would always remain constant. Something so strange, almost sinister entered their relationship. Even now she could not explain exactly what happened.

She first detected the change in Robert one evening after a teachers' meeting. He had taken the chair. Simonette sat amongst the audience, a fellow kindergarten teacher on one side, while a new teacher, a pleasant-faced young man, took the vacant seat on her left. Quite innocently and because of her inward joy, she had returned his smile and laughed at his whimsical remarks.

She had glanced up to meet Robert's heavy scowl, but had not thought seriously of the incident until after the meeting, when he had roughly taken her arm and accused her of trying to flirt with the new history master.

Her self-discipline enabled her to maintain an air of poise but her eyes could not conceal her disappointment and hurt.

"Well, what have you to say for yourself?" Robert demanded, his grip tightening.

"Robert," she whispered, "you're hurting me. Please let go of my arm."

"Don't hedge! I want the truth!"

"I was only being friendly, Robert." She needed all her poise to behave naturally. "That's all. You must believe me."

"You're sure?" He was peering at her closely. A queer light gleamed in his eyes.

"Of course! Oh, Robert – " she choked back a sob. "Don't let's quarrel. I love you! Only you. You must believe me. . . ."

"All right." Reluctantly he released her arm. "But take

care it doesn't happen again." He paused, passing a bewildered hand across his brow. "You used to be such a shy, reserved girl – sort of distant – untouched. I want to keep you that way, Simonette."

"But," she reminded him quickly, "before we met I was all alone. I'd recently lost my parents and was still missing them dreadfully. Your coming into my life was like a ray of sunshine. I began to flower again. Don't you see, darling – " she pleaded earnestly, "your love has brought me to life. I enjoy living now – life is simply glorious! Please let it stay that way. Don't try to repress me. Let me be myself. I've now discovered a new self – a self that begs for expression. Don't take it away from me. Please!"

For answer he caught her in his arms and kissed her passionately.

"It's all this waiting. . . . I just can't bear it. Marry me now, darling. Don't let's wait till the new year."

Something inside her had rebelled against the suggestion. Perhaps it was fear. She was unable to explain the sudden premonition that gripped her.

After much persuasion, Robert had agreed to wait and let the marriage take place as first planned.

But there had been no wedding – there never could be now. . . .

* * *

Wendy's high-pitched voice jolted Simonette back to the present.

"We had a lovely walk! I do feel tired. Prince enjoyed himself so much." Puffing, the child sat down on the garden chair. "I'm much too tired to walk to the station."

"Uncle Pieter will drive you and Miss O'Shea back to Sunnycove," Leila said at once, intercepting her brother's look of inquiry.

Simonette began to demur.

"It will be a pleasure, Miss O'Shea," Pieter broke in. "Just a moment while I change my shoes."

He had purposely stayed out walking longer than was expected of him. Against his will he found himself deeply attracted to Wendy's new companion.

At present marriage was not for him. Although twenty-five and old enough to marry, he had been teaching for only three years and a good deal of the money he had saved had gone toward a half share in the family car. So, being the cautious type he had at the moment no wish to become involved with any girl, much less one he could not hope to marry. Simonette O'Shea was of the Roman Catholic faith.

All the same, he told himself, here was a girl he could really learn to love – a girl he would be proud to make his wife.

Chapter Six

ON SATURDAY WENDY'S grandparents came to spend the weekend at Sunnycove. It was a sudden arrangement. They had first planned to come down sometime in February, but as Mrs. Pearson explained to her son-in-law over the telephone, February was such a hot month. Would Dean object if they moved their visit ahead a few weeks?

"Besides," Pixie Pearson had added, "Cliff and I are thinking of spending two weeks at Hermanus later in February. So if it won't be any trouble. . . ."

"Not at all," Dean had assured his mother-in-law. He smiled wryly to himself. "Pixie" – she had insisted that all her friends and relatives call her by her pet name – was probably seething with curiosity to meet Wendy's new companion.

Mrs. Pearson's face was still lovely, her hair still golden and untouched by age. Almost too young-looking to have a granddaughter of Wendy's age, Simonette mused, admiring the other's petite figure and smooth skin. Mr. Pearson, broad-shouldered with a bland smile and penetrating eyes, was a few years older than his wife. Both appeared so young and vital that Simonette could not help contrasting them with her late parents, who had been elderly and ailing ever since she could remember. They had married in the middle years and Mrs. O'Shea was well in her forties when she gave birth to her first and only child.

Pixie Pearson was a talkative woman, as Simonette soon discovered. Dean was still at the office; he worked till noon on Saturdays and had telephoned to say he'd be home for lunch.

"Let me help you," Simonette begged Martha, who was busy grating carrots for the salad.

The old servant shook her head emphatically. "I can manage. You get back to the sitting-room and keep them company."

Simonette returned to the lounge where the Pearsons were already seated, their granddaughter between them.

Simonette was startled by the child's resemblance to her grandmother. As if reading Simonette's thoughts, Mr. Pearson, with a touch of pride, remarked:

"Our late daughter was the image of her mother. They were more like sisters than mother and daughter. Now Wendy here – " patting the child's golden locks, "is growing up to resemble Sharlene in a most uncanny way. It's like having our girlie back with us again."

With a pensive smile, Mrs. Pearson pulled a photograph from her handbag.

"Our daughter Sharlene," she announced, handing the picture to Simonette.

"Let me see!" Wendy cried excitedly. "That's my mummy! Isn't she beautiful?" The child's eyes widened with enchantment. "Like an angel – Auntie Leila says Mummy is in heaven now."

Addressing Simonette, Mrs. Pearson broke in: "Had Sharlene lived, she'd have been twenty-eight next month. She was not yet twenty when she married Dean – far too young for marriage, we thought. In many ways she was still such a child."

I can well imagine, Simonette mused, for the smiling girl peeping out from the picture was as sweet and innocent-looking as a child. No wonder Dean had loved her so passionately, had almost worshiped her, so Simonette had learned from Leila. And what a ghastly shock for him when Sharlene had died in childbirth. He could not really be blamed for his bitterness. Simonette was now able to comprehend something of his strange attitude toward his child.

Martha came in wheeling the teacart. With a nod at Simonette, she suggested that perhaps Missy would like to pour the tea.

"How about going onto the terrace?" Simonette ventured, with a wistful gaze through the open lounge window.

"No, not outside!" Mr. Pearson objected. "My wife can't bear the sun. It gives her a headache."

"Not so much a headache," she declared, smiling affectionately at her husband. "I'm afraid it may ruin my complexion."

Simonette smiled at this frank admission. Unexpectedly her heart warmed toward Wendy's grandmother. The Pearsons, friendly and uninquisitive, had not bombarded her with awkward questions and for this Simonette was grateful.

"Dear Sharlene was the same," Pixie Pearson resumed, graciously accepting the tea Simonette handed to her. "She was always a delicate child. Oh, I'm healthy enough," she hastily answered Simonette's inquiring glance. "I may look delicate, yet there's nothing wrong with me, I assure you."

Pixie Pearson chatted on gaily, telling Simonette of Dean Stanton's courtship with her daughter.

"It was that Leila Terblanche who introduced them," Mrs. Pearson recounted, and for the first time Simonette perceived a hard note in the woman's voice. "We lived in the same street in Fish Hoek as the Terblanche family. Together Sharlene and Leila traveled by train to school in the suburbs. They were the best of friends and I must admit" – this was said grudgingly – "that Leila had a good influence on Sharlene, who sadly lacked confidence in herself. Leila was a year older and very mature for her age."

When Mrs. Pearson paused to sip her tea, Simonette asked: "Did your daughter also train to be a kindergarten teacher?"

"Indeed no! Sharlene would have been totally unsuitable for such a vocation. After she matriculated, she stayed at home with me. In those days we entertained quite a bit and the dear girl proved a great help to me. She had such a sweet, unselfish disposition. No wonder she had so many admirers. But Sharlene was not interested in anyone except Dean Stanton. And it was Leila who introduced them," Mrs. Pearson reiterated. "It was she who took my girlie away from me. It was she who made Sharlene turn so religious. . . ."

Simonette began to feel she'd rather not hear any more. But with determination Mrs. Pearson pursued the subject.

"Leila was a great churchgoer – she still is, for that matter. Nothing seems to shake her faith. We also attend church, but we believe in moderation. The Terblanches simply live at the church," Mrs. Pearson added with some distaste.

"Auntie Leila is taking me to Sunday school tomorrow," Wendy piped up, happy that her father had at long last agreed to let her attend.

Her grandparents exchanged perplexed glances. What had induced Dean to change his mind? Although not approving of the Terblanches' religious zeal, Mr. and Mrs. Pearson did not want their grandchild to grow up into a heathen. Previously

Dean had frowned at the suggestion that it was time Wendy was sent to Sunday school. Perhaps the new companion had something to do with the idea. Was Miss O'Shea perhaps a member of the same church as the Terblanches?

Simonette shook her head. "I'm a Catholic," she stated simply.

The Pearsons made no comment. Taking Wendy's hand, her grandfather led her out onto the terrace, while the grandmother resumed her story.

"After Sharlene passed away, we couldn't bear to go on living in Fish Hoek."

"That was understandable," Simonette murmured in sympathy.

"So we sold our house and took a flat in Clifton – that's at the other side of the Peninsula. With the aid of a good nurse, we cared for Wendy till she was old enough to attend kindergarten. Then her father wanted the child back with him again. Dean considered that it was his responsibility to bring up his daughter now that she was six years old and no longer a baby. So until recently Wendy had a succession of nursemaids. But these were most unreliable. Then Dean hit on this idea of a companion for Wendy. Besides, she's seven now and a schoolgirl. I think Wendy is fortunate to have you, Miss O'Shea," and Mrs. Pearson gave Simonette a sweet, sincere smile.

"Thank you," she whispered, deeply touched. "Won't you call me Simonette?"

"I'd be delighted!" The older woman rose to her feet. Simonette stopped in the act of placing empty cups and saucers on the teacart. Her eyes followed the other's gaze across the vast expanse of blue water.

"It is certainly lovely in this part of the world. . . ."

"Hope you won't find it too lonely, Simonette. Sunnycove is rather an isolated place – not like Fish Hoek. Where we live at Clifton it is gay and well-populated. There's plenty of life around and the beaches are always crowded on weekends. And it's so near town – only about ten minutes by car. You must come and visit us, Simonette, and bring Wendy with you, of course."

"I'd love to – "

"I'll speak to Dean about it. . . . Perhaps one afternoon next week. You must stay to dinner – I'll ask Dean to come as well – he could bring you home afterwards. It's quite a way from here. First you have to travel into Cape Town and then via Sea Point out to Clifton. I only hope he doesn't decide to bring that detestable secretary of his along – I simply can't stand the woman!"

"The same here!" Wendy cried, springing suddenly through the french windows. "I just can't stand the woman!"

"Wendy!" her grandmother remonstrated, swiftly concealing a smile. "That's not the way to speak about anyone."

"But you said it, gran. I heard you." The child stared innocently at her grandmother.

"I'm sorry, dear – I shouldn't have said it. It was quite wrong of me." She smiled placatingly.

"Didn't you mean it, gran?" Wendy furrowed her brow.

Mrs. Pearson hesitated. Then tactfully she rejoined: "How's dolly? You must show me that lovely new doll your father gave you for Christmas.

"But you've already seen her! You said what a beautiful dolly she was. She can even pinch," Wendy added with relish. "Miss de Klerk got quite a fright when dolly gave her a nip. She wants to be my new mummy, but we don't want her."

Impulsively the child caught hold of her grandmother's hand.

"Don't you think it's about time I had a new mummy?"

Startled, Pixie Pearson gazed down at her grandchild.

"Whoever's been putting such ideas into your pretty little head?"

"No one. At least no one but dolly did. She would like to have a grandmother. She told me so."

"But I'm her grannie as well as yours, darling."

"I'm dolly's mummy," the child declared proudly, "so my new mummy will be her grandmother. Don't you see?"

Wendy paused for breath. Beseechingly she turned her blue eyes upon Simonette. "I think it a good idea if Miss O'Shea agreed to become dolly's grannie. Then Miss O'Shea would be my mummy."

Astonished and disconcerted, Mrs. Pearson looked across at Simonette. But with perfect composure and without embarrassment, she spoke to the child.

"I'd be glad to be your dolly's grannie. But it's your daddy who will have to choose your new mummy. We can't do that for him, you know."

"But wouldn't you like to be my mummy?" the child persisted.

"Really, Wendy!" her grandmother objected.

"Sorry, gran, but I'd like to know."

Simonette read both concern and apprehension in the child's sweet, uplifted face.

"Of course I would," Simonette patted the child's golden head. "Any mummy would love to have you, Wendy. Now go and fetch dolly."

The child stood undecided. Then gravely she addressed her grandmother.

"You know, if Miss O'Shea had said 'no,' then I'd have asked Auntie Leila. I'm quite sure she'd love to marry daddy. I hope she won't be too disappointed."

Just then Mr. Pearson returned to the lounge and surveyed the group with some amusement.

With shining eyes Wendy looked up at him. "Such wonderful news! Miss O'Shea has agreed to be my new mummy."

"Really." Mr. Pearson's tone did not indicate whether the announcement pleased him or not.

He sought his wife's gaze. "Wendy was just going to fetch dolly. Weren't you, darling?" Pixie smiled at the child. "I'm sure dolly would love to meet her new grandmother."

Later in the day when the two were alone together, Mr. Pearson inquired of his wife: "What was all that nonsense going on in the lounge this morning, Pixie?"

She smiled wryly. "You may call it nonsense, but I wonder!" Then she proceeded to recount to her husband exactly what had taken place.

"But surely you can't take Miss O'Shea's declaration seriously? Why, the girl hardly knows Dean."

"That's true. But I wasn't thinking of Simonette as Dean's second wife."

"Not that de Klerk woman, surely?"

Pixie shook her head. "We've nothing whatever to fear in that direction. I'm quite confident Dean's feelings for her are entirely impersonal. Thank goodness he has no romantic interest in that character! No, Cliff – I'm thinking of Leila Terblanche."

With a chuckle, he exclaimed. "Leila Terblanche! Good grief, Pixie! You can't be serious? Leila's the last person I'd imagine Dean falling for. Not that she's unattractive, mind you. She has her good points – that beautiful red hair and those green eyes. But she's far too religious. She wouldn't suit Dean – "

"I wish," Mrs. Pearson broke in with a slight frown, "that Dean would seriously consider attending church again. It's good to take an interest in religion of some kind. Of course, not to the extent that the Terblanches do," she hastily amended. "That's going to extremes. I believe in moderation in all things. I'd be pleased if he came to church now and again. Churchgoing gives one a certain amount of respectability."

"Sure . . . sure. . . ." Mr. Pearson paused. "It would be a good idea if Dean did remarry – "

"Cliff!" his wife ejaculated in scandalized tones.

"Well . . . why not?" he countered. "Surely you don't expect Dean to mourn forever. Sharlene's been gone seven years now. I'm surprised he hasn't married again."

"How can you be so heartless? The dear boy loved Sharlene so much. He was absolutely devoted to her – he adored her."

Mr. Pearson nodded. "That's true. All the same, we've got to be realistic about this, my dear. One day he's bound to marry again."

"Hm . . . maybe you're right," Pixie Pearson murmured after some contemplation. "We can only hope it won't be to that Leila woman, though."

"Have no fear, my dear. If Dean were at all interested in Leila Terblanche, he'd have married her years ago. Remember, he knew her long before he met Sharlene."

"Yes, I guess you're right." Mrs. Pearson gazed admiringly at her husband. Cliff was always so sensible, so practical. . . . He exuded common sense. "You are invariably so right."

He came across to where she stood, stooped down, and kissed her tenderly.

"Dear little Pixie," he whispered fondly, stroking her golden head. "What would you do without me?"

She gave a little shudder. "Don't say that! I'd die if anything should happen to you." She stretched up and pressed her cheek against his. "God has been good to us after all. He took away our daughter, but we still have each other. We have much to thank Him for."

"Sure we have," her husband agreed heartily. "And we have the sweetest little granddaughter and a fine son-in-law."

"Dean won't be our son-in-law any longer if he remarries. He'll have new in-laws."

"All the same, we still have our grandchild. Wendy will

always belong to us. Nothing can alter that – not even Dean's marriage to another woman."

Pixie smiled tremulously. "Yes, dear, you are so right. So very right."

There was silence between them – a silence without constraint.

Suddenly Pixie exclaimed: "I've just thought of something, Cliff. Dean must marry Simonette O'Shea."

"Good grief! You're not serious?"

"I am. Terribly serious. Simonette would be ideal for Dean. She's beautiful, well-spoken, and obviously comes from a good family. She's well-educated and knows how to handle Wendy, who absolutely adores her."

"But we know practically nothing of her background – her private life – "

"Dean has told us all there is to know and I, for one, am perfectly satisfied. At least she goes to church – "

"But the girl's a Roman Catholic – "

"What does that matter? She has some semblance of religion. She's not a skeptic, like that de Klerk woman. Nor is she a Leila Terblanche." Mrs. Pearson hesitated. "Besides, I like Simonette. There is something about her. . . ."

"An air of mystery," Cliff Pearson murmured, "as the writers would say."

"What's that, dear?"

"Nothing . . . just thinking aloud. . . ."

"But don't you consider it a good match?" Somewhat anxiously Pixie looked up at her husband. "She has no parents, so there would be no problem in that direction. I'd say Simonette and Dean are ideally suited."

"Maybe, if she and Dean were attracted to each other. But there's nothing there – absolutely nothing. By the way, where is she now? I heard her ask Dean if she could go off for an hour or so."

"Simonette has gone to church."

"You don't say! Anything special on at the Catholic church this evening?" Mr. Pearson spoke with studied nonchalance. He knew full well that according to the notice board outside the church, Saturday evenings were set aside for the hearing of confessions.

"Not that I know of." His wife shrugged her slender shoulders.

Hm . . . Cliff Pearson mused. The mystery deepens. There was something definitely odd about that O'Shea girl. Beautiful she doubtless was, well-spoken and gentle, and a fitting companion for Wendy. All the same, he pursed his lips resolutely, he didn't want to see Dean married to Simonette O'Shea. She had a past, of that he was positive, and it might not be a past of which he'd altogether approve. When it came to a stepmother for Wendy, he'd prefer Leila Terblanche any day. A frank, wholesome girl. Not like that Simonette O'Shea. She was too guarded for his liking.

Cliff Pearson puckered his brow. What unsavory past did she have to confess?

Chapter Seven

It was still light when Simonette reached the little Catholic church in Fish Hoek. The days had not yet begun to shorten. Children were playing on the beaches; people were watering their parched gardens. The Cape weather was so different from that of Johannesburg where they had summer rains. In Johannesburg there were no beaches, no long, scenic drives beside the sea.

As Simonette entered the church, her mind automatically reverted to the time when perplexed, grief-stricken and terrified by Robert's queer behavior, she had fled from him and sought refuge within the church sanctuary.

She had not believed he would react so violently to her suggestion that they postpone their marriage until the winter vacation.

Somewhat breathlessly she had excused herself by saying: "I'd hate to have a wet wedding day." In the Transvaal winter time was the dry season with warm sunny days and frosty nights. Seldom did Johannesburg experience Cape Town's stormy winters, with fierce gales and lashing rain.

"What rubbish!" Robert had expostulated. "You're just making excuses again, Simonette. I've been patient for a year now. Either you marry me now – or else – "

She had waited with palpitating heart.

"– we'll call the whole thing off," he finished.

Relief struggled with bitter disappointment. She had hoped that he would agree to the postponement, that during the extra time of waiting she would learn to understand him better, that his dark moods would vanish as mysteriously as they'd first appeared, that he would again become the man to whom she had first given her heart.

She pulled at her ring with trembling fingers.

"Don't you dare touch it!" he had fairly screamed at her. "Of course I didn't mean it, you stupid girl! I want to marry you more than anything else in the world. I can't live without you, Simonette darling."

"So you will agree to the postponement, that we marry during the winter vacation instead?" she asked quiveringly.

"Of course I agree! I agree to anything you say, darling." Fervently he grasped her hand.

"Oh, Robert," she breathed, "I do love you so."

But when he started to kiss her so fiercely, so demandingly, she was again torn by conflicting emotions. Had she been wise to suggest a postponement? Wouldn't it be wiser to let him go? A marriage with fear predominating was bound to fail. She did love Robert, it was true, and he loved her. However, she had no wish to marry someone who was fast becoming a stranger to her. The wall of distrust, of suspicion that stood between them seemed to grow more insurmountable every day.

His jealousy, his explosive anger terrified her. A smile from a colleague, especially a male member of the staff, would provoke a fresh explosion of rage. She could not explain her own confused reactions. Many a time she had been stung into defending her friends, but she soon learned that it was better just to smile an apology. Each outburst on his part would leave her limp and exhausted.

She now knew that at the time she had made a grave mistake in not confiding her fears to her father confessor. But would Robert's uncle believe her fantastic story? Would anyone believe her?

Robert, who was always so charming, so polite, so meticulously correct in his behavior. No one suspected the dark side to his nature, least of all Robert's elderly uncle. Father Cunningham was the young man's only living relative.

Her marriage to Robert was to take place at the beginning of July. This was the new arrangement. But when the time came Simonette again shrank from the thought of becoming his wife.

She was a coward, she knew, in not telling him the truth that it was fear that caused her to vacillate and not fickleness, as Father Cunningham had so darkly hinted.

After the fatal accident she blamed herself bitterly for her cowardly behavior. How could she ever learn to live with herself again? she wondered, filled with anguish and remorse. She had not taken Robert seriously, had not really believed that he would carry out his vehement threats.

But was she altogether to blame for what had happened? Was she alone responsible for Robert's strange, abnormal behavior?

When she had pleaded with him to end their engagement, he stubbornly refused even to consider the idea.

"I won't let you do this to me, Simonette," his retort came angrily. "You promised to be my wife and marry me you will! I'll sue you for breach of promise if you refuse."

Forcefully he seized her shoulders with both hands. His bloodshot eyes peered into hers with an intensity that left her speechless with shock and trepidation, yet somehow she managed to maintain a semblance of self-control.

"I mean it, Simonette!" he went on relentlessly when she did not speak. "I mean every word I say. I'll sue you! Now let's not hear any more of this sort of talk. I won't tolerate it!"

His eyes were still gazing deep into hers, imposing his will upon her.

She forced herself to speak. "No. I can't do it, Robert."

"What do you think people will say when they hear I've been jilted? I'll be the laughingstock of the whole school. Please, Simonette! Do consider my feelings just a little."

"That's what I've been doing all the time, considering your feelings," she'd flung at him a trifle childishly.

"You don't love me any more," he accused her bitterly.

She hesitated, mystified and pained by his actions – and her own.

"Simonette!" Now he was holding her in his arms. He regretted his violent outburst and looked at his fiancée with the charming expression he could so readily assume.

"Please forgive me, darling. I promise to be different. Truly I do."

She moved away from his arms. "Last time you promised, it didn't make the slightest difference in your actions. No, Robert, it's just no good. You can't seem to trust me. A happy, successful marriage is based on mutual love, faith and trust. I trust you, Robert. I don't explode with jealousy – or fume inwardly either – when an attractive girl happens to greet you. I accept it as part of life. But you – " Involuntarily she shuddered. Her strange forebodings had returned. "No, Robert, marriage to you wouldn't work out. I'm so sorry – "

He was sobbing now – great convulsive sobs shook his shoulders.

"Oh, Simonette! If you won't marry me – I'll – I'll kill myself! I mean it, Simonette."

In utter consternation she stared at him and perceived the desperate, wild, fanatical glint in his eyes.

"I mean it!" Robert reiterated with force. "Just give me another chance, my darling. Just one more chance," he entreated earnestly.

And so she had relented. She could do nothing else.

All the same, she had insisted that they wait just a few months longer before marrying.

"It's all this waiting," he had grumbled. "It's enough to send a man round the bend."

Was that what had really happened, Simonette wondered. Had Robert lost his reason? Had she by her cowardice, her procrastination sent an innocent man to his untimely death? Father Cunningham had accused her of doing just that, and now she must pay the bitter penalty.

Baffled, Simonette put a hand to her burning forehead.

What would her new father confessor have to say? What would be his opinion? Would he also insist that to atone for her sin she must enter a covent? Simonette shrank from the thought.

Robert had not changed as he had promised. She had not believed he was capable of carrying out his promise.

Months before the accident, indeed a whole year before, it had dawned on Simonette that something was radically wrong with the man to whom she had given her heart. Intuitively she knew that she was not wholly responsible for the tragedy that had taken place, that there were other things involved, factors which she was unable to fully comprehend.

Sitting in the little Fish Hoek church, waiting her turn at the confessional, Simonette's mind went over the events that had taken place just prior to the catastrophe that had befallen Robert.

It had been raining heavily since lunch time that spring morning in early October of last year. October tenth was Kruger Day and a public holiday. Simonette had arranged to meet Robert that afternoon. She was desperate now, almost at breaking point.

In spite of the heavy downpour, Robert proposed that they

drive out to Zoo Lake, a popular beauty spot in Johannesburg. To humor him she had consented, though she herself would prefer a drive into the heart of the city. She was afraid to be alone with him when she told him.

For a while they sat in the car, idly watching the rain fall into the lake. Though outwardly composed, Simonette was tense and strung up. The high humidity did not add to her comfort and she was relieved when Robert agreed with her that they go and have some tea.

"Maybe you'd prefer ice cream," he suggested, leading her inside the cool, comfortable restaurant.

She shook her dark head. "I'd rather have tea." She hoped the tea would have a steadying effect on her nerves.

"Darling, I'm so happy," he breathed. His hand stole across the table to meet hers in an ardent grasp. "Just two more months and you'll be mine. I can't wait for the time to arrive."

She swallowed hard. "Robert – oh, Robert," she cried weakly.

"Simonette darling, I do love you so." His handsome face was flushed, his eyes glowed with a feverish light. "I should have married you straight after we met." His smile was rueful. "All this waiting. . . . First it was to have been January this year, then it was July. Now at last you've promised faithfully to marry me before Christmas."

"We haven't been engaged for such a long time," she reminded him. "Some couples have to wait years before being in a position to marry."

"That's not for me. Patience isn't one of my virtues, I'm afraid."

She sighed. He perceived the uncertainty in her eyes.

"What's bothering you now?" A harsh note had crept into his voice. "What game are you playing at?"

"Game?" She was shaken by his vehemence.

"Well, isn't that what you've been doing all this time? Playing hard to get."

"You mean – you think that of me?" she stammered. She took a hurried sip of tea.

Robert could not believe that any girl in her right senses would refuse to marry him. He was highly successful, intelligent, good-looking, charming. . . . What more could any woman want in a husband?

"I know I'm not exactly rolling in money." Now he was

smiling at her, the charming smile she knew so well. "But at least I can give you all the comforts you've been accustomed to."

Tremulously she responded to his smile. "I wouldn't care if you had nothing – if I loved you. . . ."

The smile vanished. "But you *do* love me!" He was staring at her incredulously.

"Of course I love you, Robert!" Her assurance came a shade too swiftly. It would have been better, she decided, if lack of love had been the stumbling block instead of this fear of him that she felt. At least then she'd have kept her promise to marry him. Lack of love would have been a slight hindrance compared to the feeling of revulsion that would sweep over her whenever he lost control of his temper. She was still smarting from his display of temper the previous day.

And last week his unrestrained emotions had nearly caused him to become involved in a fight with a man to whom she had merely smiled her thanks for retrieving a dropped parcel.

An aloof nod of the head, Robert had told her afterwards, would have been more than sufficient. She was far too free with her smiles where men were concerned. How many times had he not warned her of her disgusting behavior?

And so another stormy scene had ensued, after which Robert had been full of humble apologies.

Things simply can't go on like this any longer, she told herself wearily. If they did her nerves would finally crack up.

She was firmly convinced that Robert was the victim of incipient insanity. All the symptoms were there. The sudden changes of mood . . . the sudden and uncontrolled outbursts of temper . . . the glittering eyes. . . .

"Robert. . . ." Sympathetically she smiled at him across the table. "Remember whatever happens I shall always love you. Even though I feel I can't possibly marry you – "

He caught her hand in a grasp that hurt. "Let's get out of here!"

"No! Please – I'd like to stay." She was petrified at the prospect of driving back with him in his present mood.

He took a furtive glance around the restaurant. No one was watching.

"You're coming with me now!" was his peremptory whisper through set lips. He dug his nails into her flesh. She had no option but to follow him out of the restaurant.

The urge to flee from him was strong. Somehow she managed to walk sedately to the car. In grim silence he opened the door for her to get in. Still not speaking, he started the car.

"Where are we going?" she queried, white-faced and frightened.

"Since you refuse to marry me, we may as well die together."

Panic seized her as she perceived the wild, fanatical expression in his eyes. For a few agonizing moments she was bereft of speech.

Then she found her voice. "Please drive me home, Robert." She tried to speak normally. "This nonsense must stop!"

"It's no nonsense! We shall die together, you and I. Remember I warned you I'd kill myself if you refused to marry me. But why should you go off scot-free? You're to blame, Simonette. It's all your fault – " His voice rose frantically. "You led me on – you deserve to die!"

"No! No!" Her breath came in great gasps. "Please let me out!"

He accelerated savagely and the car sped forward.

Simonette strove to compose herself. "You're distraught, Robert. You can't possibly mean it. Let's go and see a doctor, darling. He'll be able to help you."

"There's nothing the matter with me. It's you!" Accusingly, he spat out the words. "Admit you've been playing a cat and mouse game with me. It inflated your ego to have a good-looking fellow fawning over you."

She sat frozen in her seat.

"I deny that I've been playing with your affections. At first I couldn't understand what had happened to you. Quite suddenly you were no longer the man with whom I'd fallen in love. You've changed – you've become a different person. I'm worried – desperately worried. You're ill, my darling. . . ."

He laughed gratingly. "There's nothing wrong with me! How dare you insinuate such a thing – "

"Oh, look out, Robert!"

"You mind your own business and leave the driving to me."

"I'm sorry. . . ." She was shaking violently, unable any longer to control her deep distress. "I'd like to get out. Please!" They had stopped at a traffic light.

"No, you're not!" His grip on her arm was like a vice. Then the lights turned green and the car once again shot forward in frantic haste.

Simonette felt like screaming. Instead her lips began to

move mutely in prayer. It was not often that she prayed outside the holy precincts of the church. She preferred to be in a holy atmosphere, to be surrounded by pictures of saints, to see the holy Virgin beaming blissfully down upon her.

But these external props did not seem to matter now. Simonette prayed as she'd never prayed before in her life.

God must have heard her prayer, for when the car screeched to a halt at the next red light, she flung open the door, and exerting all her strength, managed to throw herself out of the car. She escaped with a few slight bruises.

Recklessly Robert sped on to his death. . . .

Chapter Eight

EAGERLY LOOKING FORWARD to attending Sunday school, Wendy woke early on Sunday morning. Excitedly she banged on Simonette's door.

"Come in," she called drowsily, expecting to see Martha waddling in with early morning tea.

Because of her mental anguish the night before, Simonette had slept badly. She was therefore not too pleased to find it was Wendy who had awakened her so much earlier than usual.

The child opened the venetian blinds and the pearly light of dawn stole into the room. Simonette's bedside clock showed it was not yet six o'clock.

"Hope you're not cross 'cause I woke you so early." A trifle sheepishly Wendy surveyed Simonette, who was rubbing the sleep from her eyes.

"Oh, I can't wait till nine o'clock!" she continued. Auntie Leila said she'd fetch me a little past nine."

That reminded Simonette that she herself would have to leave the house about eight o'clock if she were to be in time for eight-thirty mass.

In the hall she met Dean Stanton who was clad in sports clothes.

"You're up early, Miss O'Shea. Going to mass, I presume."

She nodded. "Just as well Wendy woke me at six, otherwise I'd have slept late."

He frowned his displeasure. "I expressly told the child not to disturb you. If that isn't disobedience for you!"

"I didn't mind. . . . Really, I didn't —"

"It's not a question of minding," he retorted frostily, "but one of obedience. Wendy," her father called sternly. "Come here, will you."

"Yes, daddy?" The child was at a loss to understand what wrong she had now committed, why her father was staring at her so sullenly.

"How dare you disregard my orders! Didn't I tell you not to disturb Miss O'Shea?"

The child began to whimper. "I didn't mean to, daddy. I forgot. I was so happy thinking of going to Sunday school."

"You deserve to be punished. I've half a mind to forbid you to attend this morning."

"No! Daddy, no!" Wendy's voice rose shrilly. Sobbing convulsively she flung her arms round Simonette. "Tell daddy not to be so cruel."

Before Simonette could voice her opinion, Dean Stanton addressed her. "Do you, Miss O'Shea, consider it cruel to deprive Wendy of her pleasure?"

"I do!" Simonette spoke emphatically. "It would be an unjust punishment for such a small offense. After all, Wendy has done no harm. Punish her if you deem it necessary, but let it be a punishment to fit the offense."

"H'm. . . ." His smile was without mirth. "All right, Wendy, you may go to Sunday school. But you will forego your drive this afternoon."

"I don't mind, I'd rather go to Sunday school. Auntie Leila would have been so disappointed – "

"What's all the commotion about?" Silently the Pearsons had come upon the scene. Up late the night before, they had decided to sleep in this morning, but the disturbance caused them to don their dressing gowns and to hasten into the hall.

"Oh, gran!" Gleefully Wendy flung her arms round Pixie Pearson's neck. "I may go to Sunday school after all. Auntie Leila is calling for me."

"Then grandpa and I will come to fetch you afterwards. Won't we, Cliff?" Mrs. Pearson glanced at her husband, her eyes filled with eloquent appeal. "And we can take Wendy for a drive then instead of going out this afternoon. We can have our rest later."

So Wendy would have her drive after all! Simonette darted a glance at Dean to see how he would accept this turn of events. She fully expected him to protest, but to her surprise he merely shrugged his shoulders in seeming surrender.

As she was crossing the drive, he called out to her: "May I offer you a lift, Miss O'Shea?"

She hesitated a second, then replied, "Thank you, Mr. Stanton." It would be churlish to refuse.

Neither mentioned the incident. It took only a few minutes by car to reach the church in Fish Hoek and the journey was made in silence.

She thanked him politely, if somewhat coldly. Dean explained he was on his way to play golf but would be home for Sunday dinner. Would she be there?

She then told him that after mass she intended to take the train through to Cape Town.

After an early lunch she caught the bus to Sea Point. Mrs. Pearson had raved about the popularity of the place. Simonette was frankly disappointed. There were far too many people milling aimlessly around: the beaches were crowded; cars of every description filled the parking lots. The lawns were certainly well-kept and easy to stroll on, the flower beds gay and attractive. However, Simonette preferred the ruggedness, the splendor and solitude of Sunnycove.

Although the Atlantic Ocean was colder than the warm Indian Ocean of the False Bay, Fish Hoek side of the Peninsula, the air was considerably warmer at Sea Point. Here was no cooling southeast breeze to fan her warm cheeks. Her brimless hat did not provide any shelter from the burning afternoon sun.

So Simonette began to stroll back the way she had come. At least along the main road there was the shade provided by the shop awnings. She would have tea in one of the restaurants she'd seen earlier from the bus window.

As Simonette made her way to a vacant table, a young man jumped up from a nearby chair and confronted her.

She was too startled to stifle her gasp of dismay.

"Ken!" she cried in consternation. "Ken Mitchell!"

Robert had been a close friend of his. The last time she had seen Ken Mitchell was on the station platform in Johannesburg. He had come running alongside the train as it slid out of the station. He had shouted something to her, but Simonette had taken no heed of his cries. Her one thought had been to get away from him and all those who belonged to her past.

What was Ken doing in the Cape? In Sea Point?

Simonette did not wait to find out. Turning swiftly on her heel, she made for the door.

"Wait, Simonette! I must see you!"

Outside the restaurant was a bus stop. A bus was just about

to pass when the driver, catching sight of Simonette's raised hand, brought the vehicle to a halt with a screech of brakes. Breathlessly she clambered inside. A kindly conductor helped her to a seat.

It was absurd to panic, she chided herself severely, just because that dark shadow of the past had again risen to confront her. By the time the bus reached the city she had herself under some control.

As it was too early to catch the return train to Sunnycove, Simonette thought it a good idea to pay a visit to the public gardens at the top of Adderley Street.

She started to cross the street. Had Ken Mitchell been transferred by his firm to Cape Town? Was he down here on holiday? It was not likely that she would meet him again – Sunnycove was at the other end of the Peninsula.

Preoccupied in sorting out the warring emotions the encounter with him had stirred in her, Simonette did not see that she was going against the light until a car was almost on top of her.

Skillfully the driver avoided her and pulled the car to a standstill beside the curb. Then she and Pieter Terblanche found themselves staring at each other in surprise.

"Simonette!" he exclaimed, delight blending with the concern in his voice.

"Pieter! How good to see you." She was genuinely relieved. At least here was a friend.

Without further ado he opened the car door. Automatically she got in beside him. He gave her a searching glance.

She was pale and shaken and there were dark shadows beneath her gray eyes. He knew a pang of sympathy.

"Sorry if I startled you," he began.

"But it was my fault," she chimed in with an apologetic smile. "I should have looked where I was going. I was on my way to the gardens."

"And I'm on my way home. Directly after lunch I was called to the bedside of one of my pupils who is seriously ill in the hospital. His parents asked me to come and pray with him. The lad seemed much brighter when I left. You see, he was afraid to die. But I explained to him the way of salvation and assured him he had nothing to fear if he put his trust in the Lord Jesus Christ."

"Oh." It took a few moments for the import of this to sink

into Simonette's mind. Like his sister Leila, it seemed that Pieter also went about helping those in need. Would they be able to help her? Wonderful thought!

But no! She was a Catholic and a good Catholic did not seek spiritual aid of a Protestant, however desperate he or she was. The priest was there to help.

But a lot of comfort her new father confessor had been to her last night, Simonette reflected wryly. The inevitable convent question had again cropped up. It was true her new priest had sounded more sympathetic than Father Cunningham. But that was understandable. Robert had been that priest's nephew.

Oh, how I long for peace! Unconsciously she let out a loud sigh.

"Sorry if I upset you, Simonette." Pieter's calm, compassionate voice broke gently into her musings.

"You didn't. . . . I wasn't looking where I was going."

"Instead of arguing the toss, let's go and have some tea in the gardens. I'm absolutely parched."

She welcomed the suggestion and sank gratefully into a chair under a large, shady tree. But she did not see the velvety green lawns or the bright display of late summer blooms.

To turn her thoughts away from herself and her problems, she asked Pieter about his family and their early life in Fish Hoek. And as he spoke she became aware of the unsuspected strength and power that his shy, almost casual manner disguised.

There had been an elder brother who had died when he was Pieter's age. No, he was not a school teacher. Hugh had worked in the bank where their father was now the manager.

"Mother and Hugh were both killed in a motor accident – "

"Your mother as well!" interposed Simonette in shocked surprise. No wonder at Leila's reluctance to drive the car. "I knew, of course, that your mother was dead, but I'd no idea how she died."

"I was just nineteen – Leila a few years older. But she took over the reins like a real mother. We were glad that she was not married and was free to step into Mother's shoes, so to speak. Father and I owe a great deal to Leila."

"Your sister has not been in love – she has not thought of marriage?" The question was out before she could prevent it.

"Oh, that was tactless of me! Please forgive my asking, Pieter."

"That's all right, Simonette." He smiled spontaneously. "You must have guessed, of course."

"Well . . . not exactly. But I had an idea. She was fond of Dean Stanton, wasn't she?"

Pieter nodded. "But to him Leila was merely a good friend. In the summer vacation when he was home from the university – Dean was studying law – he used to call for Leila to take her to youth meetings." Pieter paused to drink his tea.

"You didn't accompany them?"

"Sometimes. But remember Leila's almost four years my senior. She had just started training in college; I was studying for my junior certificate. They didn't see each other often, though. Both were studying hard."

"Where does Wendy's mother fit into the picture? Mrs. Pearson has told me something of the background, but I'm afraid I wasn't listening all the time."

"No wonder! Pixie Pearson is a great talker. Has she asked you to call her Pixie yet? No? But she will, Simonette."

"Do I detect a hidden warning in your words?" Momentarily forgetting her troubles, Simonette smiled at Pieter.

He grinned. "Not at all! Leila and I are both fond of Wendy's grandparents. They're a fine couple, really. But Pixie holds it against Leila that it was she who introduced Dean to their daughter."

"Were the Pearsons against the marriage then?" Simonette poured herself a second cup of tea.

"Not exactly. They reckoned Sharlene was far too young – she was not yet twenty when she and Dean married. She was a delicate girl, very pretty, I'll admit. Can't say I blame Dean for falling in love with her."

"Were you also fond of her, Pieter?" Simonette's grave gray eyes had lost their haunted look.

Pieter chuckled. "No fear! I was deeply immersed in my studies and sports. Girls just didn't enter the picture. But even had I been older, I doubt whether Sharlene would have attracted me. She wasn't my type."

But you attract me, Simonette. Tenderly Pieter's gaze strayed across the table to the dark, slender girl sitting opposite him. There was real beauty in Simonette's face – not just mere prettiness. But it was a sad face, the face of one who had suffered greatly, indeed, was still suffering.

"Now, tell me a little about yourself, Simonette." His casual tone cloaked a deep desire to know what was causing her such sorrow, such mental anguish. He longed desperately to help her.

Watching her covertly, he saw her slight start of apprehension. Involuntarily her hands moved in a nervous gesture.

In order to put her at ease, he started to hum softly to himself.

She was swift to grasp the opportunity to steer the conversation away from herself.

"That's a lovely tune."

"You like it?"

"I do. Are there any words to it?"

He nodded. "Want to hear them? Good!"

Earnestly Pieter commenced to quote Wesley's majestic hymn.

> O for a thousand tongues to sing
> My great Redeemer's praise,
> The glories of my God and King,
> The triumphs of His grace!
>
> He breaks the power of canceled sin,
> He sets the prisoner free;
> His blood can make the foulest clean;
> His blood availed for me.

They sat for awhile in meditative silence.

"Just say that last verse again, Pieter," Simonette begged presently.

He did so, a prayer in his heart.

"Oh, if only I could believe the words are true!" The wistful note in her voice did not escape him.

"But they are true, Simonette!" Pieter spoke with a touch of urgency. "The Lord is waiting for you to let him solve your problem, whatever it is."

"Who said anything about a problem?" She was immediately on the defensive.

His gaze was steadfast, searching.

She lowered her head. "I suppose it's no use pretending any longer." She sighed loudly. "I do have a problem, Pieter – a grave problem. I'm seriously thinking of entering a convent."

"A convent!" he echoed, too astonished to check his alarm. "Oh no, Simonette – you mustn't!"

She was knotting her hands nervously. "It's the only way

out – the only solution. There at least I'll be able to find peace."

"But God can give you peace, Simonette. And you don't have to enter a convent to receive it. The Lord is our peace."

"My priest has urged me to take holy vows. It's the only way out, he thinks."

"When did he tell you this?"

"Just before I left Johannesburg for Cape Town. He said that by running away I was trying to escape the punishment of my sins. I must make expiation – "

"But the Lord Jesus has done it all! There's no need for you to sacrifice your life, Simonette." Eagerly Pieter leaned across the table, his eyes shining in earnest appeal. "The Lord has already done that for you. He died on the cross for your sins and mine."

She looked at him in confusion. "Last night when I went to confession, my new priest told me that only within the convent walls would I find rest and peace. But, oh, Pieter, – I don't feel called to be a nun." She struggled to keep the despair out of her voice. "The thought is abhorrent to me."

Pieter's relief was profound. So she had not yet consented to the priest's suggestion that she enter a convent.

"The idea revolts me. Oh – Pieter. . . ."

"Simonette. . . ." He had risen to his feet. "Let's get back to the car. We can't talk here."

"But there's nothing more to say," she protested weakly.

"Won't you give me a chance to help you, Simonette?" His gaze was filled with gentle entreaty.

"I couldn't possibly burden you with my worries – "

"It will be a pleasure to help you, Simonette. You know that, don't you?"

And as she looked into his face, his expression so sincere, so serene, she surrendered to an overwhelming urge to confide in him.

Chapter Nine

"THERE WAS AN INQUEST, of course." Simonette flinched at the memory. "The coroner's verdict was accidental death."

"You had not told the police of his threats to commit suicide?" Pieter asked, his hands resting on the steering wheel of his car.

They were sitting on the mountain side in a parking bay high above the city. Neither of them saw the calm blue waters of Table Bay, the hills of Blouberg, or the distant horizon.

"There was no point in it." Unshed tears lay on her dark lashes. "Robert may have taken his life because of me. How many times have I not tortured myself with the thought!" Always the possibility stared her in the face, challenging her, provoking her.

"On the other hand it could have been an accident. The car skidded on the wet road, striking a lamp post. When the police questioned me, I mentioned to them that we'd had a bit of a row and that my fiancé had driven off in a temper. Of course, I had to tell my father confessor the truth, but Father Cunningham didn't believe me. The picture I painted of Robert was a false one – a figment of my imagination, he said. He'd never known his nephew to act in such a revolting manner. Robert was always so courteous and considerate – he wouldn't harm a fly." Simonette shifted nervously. "But you do believe me, Pieter – don't you?" There was a note of anxiety in her voice.

"Sure, I believe you." Simonette's story had shaken him sadly. "I don't doubt a word of what you've said. Your fiancé's changed behavior, the strange, neurotic way in which he reacted, these are not altogether uncommon to me. It's happened to other people before now. I've actually come across a few cases."

"You have?" Her eyes widened in amazement.

"Yes." Pieter hesitated. He was reluctant to voice what was in his mind. It would only distress her still further.

"I find it hard to believe," she went on. "Even so, that's no help at all. Robert is dead and I'm responsible. At least, that's what the priests seem to think."

The intense emotions she'd experienced since last night were released in gentle weeping. Pieter let her cry – it was better that way.

When she had regained her composure, Pieter observed, "Even if you were partly responsible for your late fiancé's death, Christ has paid the penalty for your sin." He paused, undecided. Then he said, "As it's fairly late already, why not come along to church with me? We may as well stay in town and attend church here. We could have a bite to eat first."

"But isn't Leila expecting you home?" Simonette demurred.

"She is. But I could phone to say I've decided to stay in town. It's not the first Sunday I've attended our town church, you know."

"But I thought – " She broke off in some confusion. "You expect me to accompany you to your church?"

"That's the idea. . . ." He was smiling at her.

"But I couldn't! You know I couldn't attend a Protestant church! What would my priest say?" Simonette was unable to subdue the sudden alarm in her voice.

"You've not attended a Protestant church before?"

"Never! I wouldn't dare! Please don't ask me, Pieter."

"Very well." He sounded disappointed. "I thought you wanted spiritual help, Simonette."

"I do! There's nothing I want or need more. These last few months have been sheer torture for me. How on earth I managed to continue with my teaching till the end of the term I just don't know."

"So it was Robert's death that really convinced you to come to the Cape. But we can't escape from our thoughts, you know. We take them with us wherever we go. To flee from our problems is no solution. Your priest is right on that point." Pieter considered her earnestly. "Give God a chance to speak to you, Simonette. The Lord alone can offer you pardon and peace. It's not in the priest's power to do so. 'Come unto me, all ye that labour and are heavy laden, and I will give you rest.' Isn't that a precious promise, Simonette?" He gazed at her imploringly.

She was twisting her hands uncertainly. "I don't know what to say or think." The constant dual going on inside – it was so disconcerting, so disturbing.

"All right, Pieter," came her breathless whisper after a long pause. "I'll come with you."

"Good girl! That's the spirit." Joy and praise flooded his heart.

There wasn't much time for a large supper; instead they had a tasty snack in a small hillside café.

Somewhat refreshed by the meal, Simonette entered the church with a feeling of expectancy. It was the first time in her twenty-three years that she'd attended a Protestant church. She was afraid and yet, paradoxically, she was happy.

She and Pieter took a pew at the back of the well-filled church. She was suddenly absurdly pleased to have him for a companion. There was about him an air of stability, goodness, gentleness and something so infinitely reassuring in the sturdy set of his shoulders.

The service opened with a grand hymn of praise. Simonette, a trifle confused by her strange surroundings, failed to grasp the wonderful words of inspiration. However, as the offertory was being taken up, she turned the pages of her hymn book to the number listed next on the hymn board.

> Great God of wonders all Thy ways
> Are matchless, Godlike, and divine;
> But the fair glories of Thy grace
> More Godlike and unrivaled shine.

Deeply impressed, she read the words of the chorus twice.

> Who is a pard'ning God like Thee?
> Or who has grace so rich and free?

The next few lines stood out in bold relief.

> Pardon for crimes of deepest dye,
> A pardon bought with Jesus' blood.

There was a meditative, an almost incredulous expression on her face as she listened to the sermon.

The minister's theme was: "God – the all-powerful, the omnipotent God. He alone can heal, He alone can satisfy, He alone can set the captive free, He alone can deliver. But above all, He alone can redeem. . . ."

> My chains fell off, my heart was free,
> I rose, went forth and followed Thee!

Just to be free! Oh, what a glorious thought! Free of the memory that was haunting her – free of the sin that was torturing her. . . .

The service was so different from any kind she had ever known or could recall.

As the congregation rose to sing the closing hymn, Simonette's longing heart echoed the words of the hymn writer.

> Make me a captive, Lord, and then I shall be free.
> Help me to surrender up my sword and I shall
> conqueror be. . . .

Little was said on the homeward journey. Rounding the Fish Hoek bend, Pieter voiced the thought uppermost in his mind.

"Hope you found the service helpful, Simonette. . . ."

"I did! The church was strange, the congregation strangers, yet somehow I didn't feel out of place."

The Lord had seemed so very near. She could not recollect feeling His presence in such a way in her own church. There the various ceremonies, the priests' Latin chantings, all contrived to make God seem so distant, so unapproachable.

"I enjoyed the singing," she went on enthusiastically. Her eyes held a happier light. "The hymns were inspiring and uplifting. Some of the words just gripped me."

You have a poet's soul, mused Pieter, and then knew that he loved this lovely but lonely girl, who was anxiously searching for pardon and peace.

Perhaps you'd care to come again," he suggested hopefully, as they drew up outside the Stanton home.

"No! Please don't ask me, Pieter. I must first speak to my priest. I had no right, really, to be there."

What would her priest say on Saturday when she visited the confessional? A sudden chill clutched at Simonette's heart.

Before Pieter could comment, she had jumped out of the car. "Thank you for the lovely afternoon and evening. Goodbye, Pieter."

The note of finality in her voice disturbed him. But with a prayer on his lips he drove away.

The lounge light was on, so Simonette looked inside the room to see whether the Pearsons were still up. But only Dean sat alone in the large room. He glanced up from his book as she entered.

"Hope you weren't waiting up for me," she began lamely.

He took off his reading glasses and surveyed her critically. "No, I was not. Would you care for some tea, Miss O'Shea?"

She shook her head. "No, thanks. I'll just go straight to bed. It's been a long day."

"Thought I heard a car – "

"Yes. Pieter Terblanche brought me home. It's quite a distance from Cape Town to Fish Hoek, even by car. Pieter and I met accidentally near the gardens. Then Pieter invited me to church. . . ."

Dean's brows raised in surprise, his lips curled cynically. And as Simonette met her employer's hard, haughty stare, she wondered what the Dean of long ago had been like for Leila to have loved him.

Did she still love him? Leila – whose faith, despite disappointment and sorrow, had remained firm and unshaken. Leila, who was always so bright and cheerful – a testimony to those around her.

Simonette bade Dean a brief goodnight, then quickly retreated to her room, wondering whether she would ever learn to like her hard, unsympathetic employer.

Dean switched off the light and walked reflectively to his room, wishing he had the courage to do what Simonette O'Shea had done. She, a Roman Catholic, had attended a Protestant church. That must have taken a good deal of courage.

Could it have been desperation that had driven her to enter the house of God?

Chapter Ten

All through the week the memory of the church service she'd attended with Pieter Terblanche stayed in Simonette's mind. The simplicity of the service, the deep reverence pervading the atmosphere, had moved her profoundly.

It was so different from what she'd imagined or expected. No pictures of saints or the Madonna with Child decorated the walls of the church. There were no candles, no incense; no mention was made of purgatory, or the Assumption of the Blessed Virgin. The minister did not refer to the celebration of Mass, the hearing of confessions, the use of indulgences. Several members of the congregation had carried Bibles, Pieter included, and had followed the Scripture reading for themselves.

Later in the week Simonette took Wendy to visit the child's grandparents in Clifton. The weather had changed to a northwesterly wind. A fresh breeze came sweeping off the sea; puffs of dark cloud were curling around Lion's Head.

"A sure sign of rain," Pixie Pearson pointed out to Simonette. "I wouldn't be at all surprised if it rained toward evening."

The Pearson's luxury flat was on the top floor with a magnificent view over the Atlantic Ocean from the front windows. Lion's Head and the famous mountain range known as the Twelve Apostles, could be clearly seen from Wendy's old room as well as from the kitchen window.

Mrs. Pearson did her own cooking. The flat was serviced, so she did not require a maid. When she didn't feel in the mood for preparing a meal, she and her husband would dine in the restaurant on the ground floor.

"It's most convenient living here," she went on. "It's only ten minutes or so by car to Town. We can travel either via Sea Point or through the Glen over Kloof Nek. That's the quickest way if you want to avoid the traffic."

Pixie paused to consider Simonette with disarming curiosity.

"My word, Simonette, you were a little late getting back on

Sunday night. Poor Dean was becoming quite anxious in case you'd got lost or had decided not to return after all. We had to leave Sunnycove by nine o'clock, and we didn't want to be too late getting home, so we couldn't wait for you. At Sunnycove it's not quite safe for a woman to walk alone from the station at night."

"I had a lift back – "

Mrs. Pearson's eyes were frankly inquisitive. "I thought you said you didn't know anyone here on the Cape."

"Pieter Terblanche brought me back," Simonette rejoined with candor. "We met accidentally in Town."

"I'd no idea you knew him. . . ." Pixie murmured.

"I met him at Leila's last week. Wendy and I had tea there."

Mrs. Pearson did not comment. However, when later her husband, who was a company director, returned from his office and joined her in the kitchen, she couldn't refrain from expressing her thoughts.

"That Simonette O'Shea is a fast worker. In my opinion the shy ones are the sly ones. If Dean doesn't wake up, he may find himself looking for another companion for Wendy. He took practically no notice of Simonette during dinner."

"Now don't sound so disappointed, my dear," Cliff Pearson consoled his wife. "Give the boy time. Don't rush him. Don't be in too much of a hurry to get him married to Simonette O'Shea – you may regret it."

Pixie appeared crestfallen.

"Quite candidly, my dear," her husband continued, "I wouldn't like to see Dean married to that O'Shea girl. We know so little of her background. She's adept at changing the conversation when one tries to question her."

"So I've noticed." Pixie sighed. "Oh dear! I wish I knew what was best. I'd hate to see Dean turn to that Leila Terblanche. Cliff," his wife hesitated, "do you think there might be something between Pieter Terblanche and Simonette? Perhaps it's a case of love at first sight – "

Cliff Pearson chuckled. "Don't let your imagination work overtime, my dear. From what I know of the Terblanche boy, he's fairly sensible and not likely to lose his heart to the first pretty girl he meets. Besides, Simonette O'Shea is a Roman Catholic, so marriage would be quite out of the question between her and Pieter. Now, don't look so worried, my dear. Next week we're off to Hermanus, remember. So cheer up! I love you best when you're smiling." And he caught his wife in a tender embrace.

"Dear Cliff," she murmured fondly, "you are always so right. So right. What on earth would I do without you?" Childlike she raised her face for his kiss.

He closed his eyes to hide his amusement.

"It was a delicious dinner, darling. I thoroughly enjoyed it. And I'm sure Dean and Miss O'Shea did, too."

It was a long time since Simonette could recall spending such a delightful social evening. The Pearsons were certainly good company. After dinner Dean shed his reserve and chatted freely, while she herself drew confidence from the knowledge that she looked her best.

Wendy, always happy to be with her beloved grandparents, behaved like the pleasant, lovable child she really was. The evening was so different from the one she'd first spent in Dean's company, when Olivia de Klerk had also been present.

The threat of rain was imminent as they drove away from Clifton, Wendy snuggling down under a blanket on the rear seat, Simonette sitting in the front with Dean. He took the short cut through the Glen and over the Kloof to De Waal Drive. At Newlands he swung down to the main road.

It was now raining hard and the windshield wiper kept up its monotonous beat. But Dean handled the car with ease and drove confidently through the pelting rain, which seemed as though it would never cease.

It was not altogether unusual, Dean explained, to have such a heavy downpour at the beginning of February. Especially after a hot, dry summer. "Actually, this is our hottest month," he added. "February can be a real scorcher."

Simonette found she was shivering slightly. Rain always reminded her of Robert's accident, and once again pictures of the past rose up to haunt her.

Dean had the impression that the girl sitting so demurely at his side was not really listening. She was certainly a strange character, this Simonette O'Shea, who so often seemed to be locked in a world of her own. What secret was she striving so carefully to conceal?

Tomorrow was Saturday. Perhaps during the afternoon he'd find an opportunity to call at the Terblanche home. Pieter was sure to be out doing some kind of sport. It was no use asking Pieter anything – he could be as close as a clam. It was Leila

Dean wanted to see. Maybe she'd learned something about Simonette during the girl's visit last week.

Cliff Pearson's remarks earlier in the evening had disturbed Dean.

While the two women were washing up in the kitchen, Cliff commented, "Fine-looking girl this Simonette O'Shea. Know anything of her background?"

"Only what I've already told you." And Dean shrugged.

"She has pleasant manners, but one is conscious of a reserve – a withdrawal from any personal contact."

"That's my impression too." Dean nodded reflectively.

"Is she engaged to be married – or maybe she has been married before?"

"No to your second question. And as to the first I haven't the faintest notion. There could be a fiancé waiting for her in Johannesburg, though. Rather an ex-fiancé. She keeps feeling for the ring that is no longer on her finger. And that tragic expression in her eyes – " Dean finished with an eloquent gesture.

"Hm. . . ." Mr. Pearson nodded expressively. "Miss O'Shea has a past, of that I'm quite positive." He rose to draw the curtains, shutting out the fast approaching darkness. "Perhaps she is in some sort of trouble."

"Could be." Dean smiled at his father-in-law. "But remember, like the doctor or minister of religion, I'm accustomed to dealing with people who have skeletons in their cupboards. As a lawyer, I've heard many tragic stories – some none too savory, either. But I shouldn't think Miss O'Shea would have anything bad to hide. I reckon she's been downright unfortunate, the same as myself."

Cliff Pearson, contemplating the younger man's face, saw the bitterness in his eyes, the cynical twist to the lips.

"Don't you think, my boy, it's high time you put the past behind you? It's seven years now since Sharlene passed away. One can't go on grieving forever, you know."

Dean's smile was without mirth. "You've said that before, Cliff. And I agree with you. Since the beginning of the year, I've seriously been taking stock of myself. I've been a senseless fool dwelling in the past. Instead of engaging a companion for Wendy, it would be a far better idea if I got myself a wife – so Pixie tells me."

"You're not thinking of marrying again?"

"Why not? Pixie would be delighted, I know."

"It all depends upon the lady you choose. You're not considering Miss O'Shea, surely?" Mr. Pearson quickly veiled his expression.

Dean laughed. "At present I have no one in mind. But why not Simonette O'Shea? She'd be ideal. She's beautiful, gentle and good. And Wendy adores her. I'm sure Pixie would approve of my choice."

"Maybe, but if I were you I'd think twice before considering Miss O'Shea as a future wife. For one thing, she is a Catholic. Then there's her past – "

"Which I'm certain is not a murky one." Dean's interjection was a trifle dry.

"But what if it is?" his father-in-law challenged him. "Why not find out? I'm curious to know myself. And so is Pixie. Apart from the question of matrimony, we can't say we exactly care for our granddaughter to be looked after by someone of a questionable character."

"You don't like her?"

"I wouldn't say that," Mr. Pearson rejoined smoothly. "She seems a pleasant enough girl. But I'm thinking of Wendy. . . . These evasive, closed-up sort of people – " he gestured, "well, they're not exactly my type."

But you, Cliff Pearson, mused Dean, *can be pretty closed-up yourself when the occasion demands. And so can I.*

When his wife and Wendy's companion joined them in the lounge, Mr. Pearson watched his son-in-law furtively. But there was nothing in Simonette's or Dean's behavior to suggest they were at all interested in each other.

Cliff Pearson grunted inwardly with satisfaction.

The next day Dean phoned Leila from his office to inquire whether he might call on her that afternoon.

"Of course, Dean! With pleasure." Leila was aware of a quickening of her pulse. It was a long time since Dean Stanton had called on her. Not since she'd introduced Sharlene Pearson to him – and that was nine years ago – had he bothered to call especially to see her.

The thought hurt. However, Leila was not one to allow hurt pride to surmount the love which still lurked in her heart for him.

But she was absolutely determined not to allow herself to be hurt a second time.

Chapter Eleven

LEILA'S SMILE WAS WARM with welcome. The bright afternoon sunshine caressed her red hair and transformed it into a living flame. Dean had forgotten how lovely her smile was, how radiant her hair.

Leila peeled off her gardening gloves. "Last night's rain was most welcome. See how the lawn grass is shooting? Would you like to go indoors, Dean, or would you prefer to sit out here on the veranda?"

"Let's sit down here," he suggested. "It's not too hot outside."

"Have you had afternoon tea?"

He nodded and seated himself on a wicker chair. "We had tea just before I came away. All by yourself, Leila?"

"Dad's in his room resting. And, of course, Piet's out at some school cricket match. Do you still play golf?"

"Yes, but mostly on Sunday mornings." There was a touch of defiance in his voice.

"That's why I missed you on Sunday when I came to fetch Wendy to Sunday school."

"I don't usually leave quite so early, but I took Miss O'Shea to mass first." He paused a trifle awkwardly. "It was good of you to fetch Wendy, but in the future I'll run her to Sunday school before going off to golf. I don't see why you should have all that bother, Leila."

"But it's no bother, Dean, really it isn't – "

"All the same I feel it my duty to take Wendy to Sunday school." Dean spoke gravely; no mockery was in his voice, no caustic note.

If she was surprised at his change of tune, Leila did not show it. In her heart she rejoiced. If only she could establish contact with him again!

After some general conversation interspersed with restrained silences, he remarked, "I actually called to see you about Simonette O'Shea."

Leila's heart lurched in sudden disappointment. So Dean's visit was not a friendly call after all. It was no wish to renew an old friendship. She gave herself a mental shake before speaking.

"In my opinion Simonette is the ideal companion for Wendy."

"You think so? You're not merely being kind?" he asked.

"Certainly not! When it comes to the care of the young, one can't be too careful. The wrong influence can do irreparable harm."

"I heartily endorse your words." Meditatively Dean drummed his fingers on the arm of his chair. "One cannot be too careful. That's why I've come to see you about Miss O'Shea. Maybe you'll be able to throw light on something that is puzzling me."

"But surely Simonette told you about herself when she applied for the post?"

"Only what was strictly necessary."

"There's nothing odd about that," Leila put in sensibly. "She's a reserved girl – not an extrovert like me." Leila gave Dean a winsome smile. But his gaze was on the collie dog sleeping placidly at his feet. "Surely you didn't expect Simonette to bare her heart to you?"

Dean's head jerked up to see whether Leila was laughing at him. But her green eyes held a thoughtful expression, so he bit back his curt retort.

Since he didn't reply, Leila resumed, "When you employed Simonette, you didn't say anything of your personal life – "

"Definitely not!" Dean's eyes flashed indignantly. "The idea is absurd! I'm the employer – not the employee."

"All the same, a girl like Simonette, however desperate she might be to secure a post, would have turned it down if she did not consider you a suitable employer."

"You have something there, Leila." Her disarming frankness made him feel strangely ashamed. "I daresay by now Miss O'Shea has learned all about me from Pixie. Anyway, I'm thankful that she did accept the position – she gets on famously with Wendy. A little lax perhaps – but I daresay that's on account of her youth. Miss O'Shea is only twenty-three."

"Somehow I thought she was older," Leila observed, though not unkindly. "She has a sad expression for one so young. Simonette has been through some suffering, that's for sure."

"Like me?" Dean winced inwardly as he recalled the agony of the days that had followed Sharlene's death.

"I wasn't referring to you at all." Leila spoke with characteristic candor. "But now that we're on the subject, let's face facts. In some respects you brought your own suffering upon yourself, Dean. Yet all these years you've been blaming God . . . refusing to enter His house. . . ."

"I didn't expect you to be so unsympathetic."

"No doubt you didn't." Leila gave him a strange, unfathomable look. "When Sharlene passed away, I was almost as shocked and grieved as you were. But how could you be so unjust as to blame the Lord for what happened? When we stray out of His will, we are so apt to put the blame on God instead of on ourselves. It is so very convenient."

"Are you suggesting that I was out of God's will in marrying Sharlene?" Dean shot out vehemently.

"I'm not suggesting anything of the kind. But you were not unaware of her delicate health when you married her."

For a long while Dean sat in meditative silence. Leila had hit the nail on the head, so to speak. He had rebelled against God's dealings with him, and he knew when he married Sharlene, he'd not been in the center of God's will. First love, so demanding, so insistent, yet so often unreasonable, had swept him completely off balance. He and Sharlene had not sought counsel of the Lord. Both had taken it for granted that because they loved each other so desperately, God had meant them to marry. But had He?

"Hope I didn't offend you, Dean?" Leila spoke matter-of-factly.

He made no immediate reply. What had come over Leila? She was gay certainly, and also gentle and compassionate. But, he supposed, giving her a wry smile, one sometimes has to be cruel to be kind.

Not wishing to pursue the discussion, Dean turned again to the subject of Wendy's companion.

"We all dined at the Pearsons' last night. Miss O'Shea took Wendy there in the afternoon. I drove over after work. It was some remark of Cliff Pearson's that made me phone you this morning." Dean hesitated. "But now, I guess it doesn't matter."

"So it was about Simonette that you wanted to see me?" Leila was aware of acute disappointment.

Dean nodded. He fidgeted in his chair.

"What exactly do you wish to know?"

"Well. . . ." he hesitated. "She and Wendy came here to tea. Perhaps Miss O'Shea mentioned to you something of her past life in Johannesburg. Why is she so unhappy? Is she in some sort of trouble?"

Leila shrugged. "I wouldn't know. We tried to draw her out – "

"We?" Dean lifted his brows inquiringly.

"Piet came home early that afternoon – "

"Did he now?" Leaning back in his chair, Dean regarded Leila through narrowed eyes.

She was swift to detect the caustic note in his voice.

"You think Piet is running after the girl?" Leila asked bluntly.

"Could be. . . . It wouldn't surprise me in the least."

"What makes you say that?"

"He drove Miss O'Shea back to Sunnycove last Sunday night. They had been together most of the afternoon and evening."

Leila's expression betrayed her astonishment.

"So you didn't know?" Dean smiled at her obvious confusion.

"Are you sure, Dean?"

"Positive. I heard the car and their voices. Then Miss O'Shea mentioned the matter herself. She was quite candid about it."

"I haven't seen Simonette to speak to all this week. Somehow I had the impression that she was avoiding me. Now I know why."

"Because she was with your brother? No, Leila, we mustn't jump to conclusions. I daresay she's thoroughly ashamed of herself by now for attending a Protestant church – "

"You mean to say she went with Piet to church?" Leila's voice rose in amazement. "And Piet hasn't said a word to me! We've always shared things – it's not like him to be secretive."

"You are displeased?"

"No. Not at all," Leila replied promptly with emphasis. "I'm glad – very glad indeed. It's an answer to prayer. But I wish Piet had confided in me that he was taking the girl to church."

"In fairness to Miss O'Shea, I must tell you that she and Pieter met in Town quite by chance."

A frown creased Leila's smooth skin. "Piet phoned to say he wouldn't be coming home for supper – he would be attending evening worship in Town. But he didn't mention having Simonette with him. She was probably waiting in the car. Wonder why Piet hasn't said anything to me?"

"Your little brother is growing up, Leila," Dean declared drily. "When I was Pieter's age I was a married man. Isn't it time your brother gave a thought to marriage? He's almost twenty-six now."

"Don't think I'm against Piet getting married. Dad and I would love to see him happily settled down. But if he should lose his heart to Simonette. . . . You forget, Dean, Simonette is a Catholic. There could be no future for them together – only heartbreak. Oh, why did I suggest that he join us for tea that afternoon! Come to think of it, he hasn't been the same since."

As Leila paused for breath, Dean put in, "Then there's the girl's unknown past. She could be in some sort of trouble, you know. It wouldn't surprise me in the least. We must endeavor to find out what exactly is the matter with Miss O'Shea. For both Pieter and Wendy's sake – Oh, here's your brother now."

Serious and serene as usual, Pieter parked the car and strolled toward the pair seated on the veranda.

"Hullo, Dean! Good to see you again." Pieter greeted the older man cordially.

Leila's face was unusually solemn and thoughtful.

"Anything wrong?"

"Not exactly. . . . But come and sit down while I mix a cool drink for you."

Pieter took a seat next to Dean. "I'm not particularly thirsty, Leila. I had a cool drink before I left. Now tell me what has happened."

"Dean called to see me about Simonette – "

"Simonette? Has anything happened to Simonette?"

Pieter paled under his tan. Leila, studying her brother, perceived the agitation under the outward calm.

Poor Pieter! He loves her! Dear Lord, don't let him get hurt. . . .

"There's nothing wrong, really," she promptly assured her brother. "It's just that Dean had an idea we might know something about her – about her life in Johannesburg, that is. After all, she is Wendy's companion. . . ." Leila's voice trailed off uncertainly.

Pieter looked straight at Dean, his expression enigmatic. "You're not to worry. Wendy couldn't have a better companion."

"Perhaps not." Coldly Dean returned the younger man's gaze. Pieter's serenity, his masculine strength riled him. "Miss O'Shea has excellent qualifications, I know. She is trustworthy and conscientious. I'm not questioning her ability to handle children. But there is her past life. We know so very little about that." Dean moved restlessly in his chair. "Perhaps you'd be able to enlighten us, Pieter."

"Maybe I could . . . but then I'd be breaking a confidence."

"You were out with Simonette on Sunday," Leila spoke gravely, a hint of accusation in her voice.

Pieter nodded, a strangely withdrawn expression on his face. "So I was. We met by chance in Town. And yet, was it by chance? I think the Lord planned it so that I should meet Simonette. She was in a most distressed state of mind. I persuaded her to attend church with me. No doubt you heard me bring Simonette home last Sunday, Dean."

The older man nodded without speaking.

Turning to his sister Pieter apologized for not mentioning the matter to her. For a few days he had debated whether to tell Leila of his meeting with Simonette, and what she had disclosed to him about her past. He finally decided against saying anything to Leila. Though the dearest of sisters, she was somewhat of a chatterbox and might, though quite unwittingly, let something slip. Besides, he had given his promise to Simonette. Of course, Pieter chided himself, he needn't have been quite so cautious. He could have just casually mentioned his meeting with Simonette, that she had accompanied him to church. He could have asked Leila to join him in prayer for the unhappy girl.

Since Sunday he had waited patiently to hear from her. But he had waited in vain. By now, no doubt, she'd have been warned by her father confessor to have no further contact with one of the Protestant faith.

He continued to pray daily for the girl, that the light of the glorious Gospel would penetrate her darkened mind and that she'd be set at liberty from superstition and fear. Oh, that she might find the Savior who alone could release her from the guilt of the past.

After a lengthy silence, Dean said: "You'd be wise, Pieter, to tell us all you know about Miss O'Shea."

Stubbornly he shook his head. "That would be breaking a confidence. But let me assure you, Dean, that as far as Wendy is concerned you have nothing at all to fear. Simonette O'Shea is not a criminal – she has a good, clean record."

"I'm not suggesting she hasn't," the lawyer cut in curtly.

"But – Piet – can't you say what's wrong with Simonette?" Leila entreated earnestly. "The girl needs help, that's fairly obvious. Is she in some sort of trouble?"

Pieter pondered a long moment. "I can tell you this – Simonette has suffered much. A few months back her fiancé was killed in a car crash."

"Ah!" Dean gave a sharp exclamation. "I thought as much. She keeps feeling for the ring that is no longer on her finger."

"No wonder she has a sad expression," Leila murmured compassionately. "She must have loved him very dearly – "

"But there's something else bothering the girl," Dean broke in sharply. "Isn't that so, Pieter? You may as well tell us the rest." He flung the younger man a penetrating look.

Unwaveringly and without speaking, Pieter met Dean's piercing gaze.

"Yes, please do, Piet." There was concern in Leila's voice. "It's not just curiosity."

"I'm sorry, Leila. I'm not prepared to say any more. In time Simonette will tell you her story herself." Pieter turned to Dean. "I hope you are satisfied?"

The lawyer rose to his feet. "I suppose I shall have to be." There was a bitter edge to his voice.

He knew a stab of professional jealousy. Simonette had confided in the younger man instead of in himself. After all, Pieter was merely a young high school teacher accustomed to handling boys, while he was a reputable lawyer used to dealing with men and women seeking legal aid.

There was no denying it – Dean's lips twisted wryly – that whereas he dealt with law cases, Pieter knew how to help those in spiritual need. Men and women came to Dean for legal advice, but not once in the past eight years had he endeavored to aid any of his clients in a spiritual way.

He was conscious of a heaviness within as he walked to his car, Leila at his side.

Sensing his disappointment, she rested her hand on his

sleeve. "I wouldn't worry any more, Dean." Her voice grew tender. "Part of the puzzle has been cleared up, so your mind should be set at rest. Wendy couldn't have a more suitable companion than Simonette."

He smiled at Leila's attempt at consolation. In his younger days he'd often come to her with his difficulties and problems.

"Sorry you can't stay to supper, Dean."

"I must be getting back. There will be no one to take care of Wendy. Martha is off tonight and Miss O'Shea has asked to be released from duty this evening. No doubt she wants to attend the confessional, as usual." And Dean shrugged significantly. "She'll have to confess to attending a Protestant church service."

Leila nodded mechanically, her thoughts not on Simonette.

She watched Dean drive away, deeply regretting her inability to establish contact with him again.

Just what did you expect? she asked herself, stifling a sigh. *Emotionally Dean is far away from you.*

It was no use to go on hoping that the friendship she and Dean had enjoyed so long ago could ever be recaptured.

Chapter Twelve

ON WEDNESDAY AFTERNOONS it was customary for Dean Stanton to play golf, but today he returned home early to work on an important brief.

"On no account do I want to be disturbed," was his curt order to Simonette, as he firmly closed his study door.

She took Wendy to play outside on the front lawn. Although it was now the middle of March, the signs of autumn had not yet fully appeared. The sun was still warm; on some days it could be blazing hot, but the days were growing visibly shorter. Several plants and shrubs still hung onto their summer blooms while evergreen trees stood dressed in all their splendor.

Wendy's musical voice joined the gentle song of waves on the foamy shoreline below. Simonette glanced up from the book she was reading to smile in fond amusement at the child cradling her doll to sleep in her arms.

For some time she pranced restlessly up and down the lawn, cooing tenderly to her doll before placing it in the buggy. Fussily she tucked the blankets around it.

"Dolly's asleep now," Wendy whispered to Simonette. "Please don't wake her."

All was silent for awhile and when Simonette next glanced up from her book, Wendy was nowhere to be seen.

Simonette rose quickly and walked round the side of the house in search for her charge.

Dean's study window was partly open. Wendy's voice, raised in petulant anger, came clearly to Simonette's ear.

"I want a little puppy! You said when I was older I could have a puppy – "

Filled with consternation, Simonette hastened indoors, just in time to hear Dean's indignant retort.

Catching sight of Simonette, he stopped speaking. He took off his reading glasses and surveyed her with frosty disapproval.

"Can't say I exactly care for the way you're looking after my daughter. Such lack of discipline!" His dark brows drew together in displeasure. "I gave you strict instructions not to be disturbed."

"I'm sorry, Mr. Stanton," Simonette murmured, a warm color of embarrassment suffusing her cheeks. "It won't happen again, I assure you."

"It wasn't her fault," Wendy chimed in, her independent spirit rearing its head. The child reached out a hand to Simonette.

"Be quiet, Wendy!" Dean snapped, an unyielding expression in his eyes. "If I catch you coming in here again you'll get a spanking."

"But, daddy, about that puppy – "

"Not another word!" Dean sternly admonished his daughter. "Now out you get!" He was impatient to get on with his work.

"Come along, Wendy," Simonette pleaded, giving her employer an apologetic smile.

But the child wriggled her hand free and defiantly faced her father.

"You said I could have a puppy!" Suddenly she held out an imploring hand. "Please, daddy! I do so want a puppy."

"But you have your doll. Surely that's enough?" Although he spoke on a softer note, it did not altogether hide the asperity in his voice.

"I want something that is warm and alive – something that wriggles. Susan has a puppy – this morning it followed her to school."

"I don't care who has a puppy! You're not getting one." Dean regarded his daughter with irritation. "You may have a cat if you wish," he added, seeing the blue eyes well up with tears.

"Don't want a kitty! They scratch."

Her father sighed in exasperation. "That's enough, Wendy. Out you go! I have work to do." He flung Simonette a reproving glance. "Please take Wendy out, Miss O'Shea."

"Let's go to the beach, Wendy," Simonette suggested, clutching the child's hand resolutely in her own. "May I take Wendy to Fish Hoek beach, Mr. Stanton?"

"You may." Reluctantly Dean nodded in approval. "But

please don't stay out too long. I have an appointment directly after dinner, so be sure to be back in time." He waved an impatient hand.

"We will," promised Simonette solemnly, glad to escape out of her employer's study. If it weren't for the child, she would have handed in her notice weeks ago.

But Wendy needed her. Besides, she'd grown quite fond of the motherless little girl, who was starved of a father's affection. How could Dean fail to see that it was the child's hunger to be loved that was causing her to react so rebelliously?

As Simonette led Wendy away, the child began to wail unrestrainedly. "I hate him! I hate him!" she sobbed wildly. "He doesn't love me at all. He's a nasty, horrid man!"

"Shh! You mustn't say things like that about your father." Although inwardly echoing Wendy's words, Simonette was shocked by the vehemence in the child's voice. "Here, let me dry your eyes. There, that's better. Just think of the many children who haven't any father."

"You're sticking up for him – you're taking his part." Fiercely the child rubbed her eyes and glared accusingly at her companion. "He said I could have a puppy."

"When was this?"

"When he took me away from gran – when I came here to live with him. He said he'd give me one when I was older. But he didn't mean it!" And Wendy burst into a paroxysm of fresh weeping.

Simonette, moved by the hopelessness in the child's voice, caught the disconsolate figure to her.

"Hush, dear, don't cry." Soothingly she stroked the golden curls. "One day you'll be glad daddy changed his mind. You mustn't think he didn't keep his promise. Daddy changed his mind for your own good. You see, Wendy, there are some dogs that bite. Your daddy didn't want to risk your getting hurt. I'm sure Auntie Leila will agree with me."

"But the Terblanches have a big dog. I just want a tiny one." The child made a pathetic gesture.

"You forget all puppies grow up one day. Every day they get bigger and bigger. Now, come on, Wendy," Simonette spoke briskly, "wheel your dolly's buggy inside and let's get down to the beach. As a special treat, I'll take you down the steps."

"Oh, goodie!" Wendy clapped her hands in delight. "Daddy

won't let me go down the steps on my own. One day I must try to count them. There must be hundreds and hundreds."

"There's no time to count them now. But one day we will."

"Promise?"

"I do," and Simonette gravely nodded her head. "And you must promise faithfully that you will never try to go down the steps on your own."

"Do you think my daddy loves me?" Wendy anxiously asked Simonette, as hand in hand they made their way along the path known as the catwalk. Actually it was named "Jager's Walk."

The sea lapped soothingly against the side. Laughing children scrambled over rocks and splashed gleefully in the natural swimming pools created by huge boulders. On the mountain side of the walk were benches with the over-spreading branches of trees supplying some shelter from the hot afternoon sun.

"Of course your daddy loves you! But you can't expect him to be pleased when you constantly disobey him."

"I don't mean to – really I don't! I try so hard to please him. But when he takes no notice of me, then I want to annoy him. Auntie Leila says that if I gave my heart to Jesus then I'd be different." The child paused and gazed earnestly up into Simonette's face. "Have you given your heart to the Lord?"

The direct question momentarily nonplussed Simonette. Had she given her heart to the Lord? The expression was a little strange to her. She could not recollect her priest ever having asked her such a question.

"Have you, Auntie Simonette?" The child stood still while she waited for her answer.

Simonette's brow was furrowed in thought. "I can't quite remember, Wendy. But somehow I don't think I have."

"You'd know it if you had, wouldn't you?"

"I guess so. . . ."

"You'd know here." Gravely the child touched her heart.

For no reason at all Simonette was suddenly ashamed to meet the child's candid gaze.

"Auntie Leila gave her heart to Jesus many years ago. And so did Uncle Pieter. One day when I'm older I shall also give my heart to the Lord. Auntie Leila says I should do so now – " Wendy gestured with her free hand. "But sometimes I like to be naughty."

Simonette smiled inwardly at this frank admission. *Don't we all?* she mused, kicking a pebble out of the way.

"Look! There's Uncle Pieter!" Wendy gave a jubilant shout. "And Prince."

The sandy-haired young man came striding toward them, holding a collie on a leash.

Simonette and Pieter stared at each other – he, obviously delighted to meet her again; she, concealing her confusion as best she could.

"Simonette! What a wonderful surprise," Pieter exclaimed in pleasure.

"Hullo, Pieter." She strove to keep her voice casual.

"Haven't seen you for ages," he went on, regarding her quizzically. "Not since that Sunday you came with me to church."

She glanced away from his intent gaze. Deliberately she focused her attention on Wendy, who was gingerly patting the collie.

"When may I have the pleasure of taking you again, Simonette? This Sunday?" The hopeful note in Pieter's voice did not escape her.

"You know I can't possibly come with you again." She was determined not to allow his persistence to disturb her.

"You mean because of your priest?" With purpose he pursued the subject. "Come with me this Sunday." The haunted, unhappy expression still lurked in her eyes. "Please, Simonette!"

Surprised at the fervor in Pieter's voice, she gave him a dubious smile. Though she had been so emphatic in refusing his invitation, she knew deep down that she would dearly love to attend another service. But there was her priest, her father confessor to contend with.

"You know I can't, Pieter." Unconsciously she passed a perplexed hand across her forehead.

Why had she asked Dean if she might take Wendy to Fish Hoek beach? Had she come here because something inside compelled her, because subconsciously she hoped to meet Pieter here? She tried to analyze her feelings, but only succeeded in confusing herself further.

The serious expression in Pieter's face relaxed suddenly into a warm smile.

"Come, let's sit down here on this bench for awhile." He took her arm and guided her to a seat.

At his touch an unexpected warmth, a sweetness flowed through her.

But this is absurd! she told herself angrily.

He sat down beside her and inclined his head to admire the clear lines of her profile, the graceful sweep of her hair. But it was the sadness of her expression that stirred him deeply.

How he longed to help her! He yearned with all his heart that she would come to know the Lord who was the source of all true peace and joy, that she would learn to put her complete trust in Him who alone had power to grant forgiveness to a soul bogged down by guilt and grief.

Chapter Thirteen

THE SUN WAS SLOWLY MOVING westerly across the cloudless sky; the blue waters shimmered in the slanting rays; waves rolled lazily to wash the silvery sand.

"Oh my!" ejaculated Simonette in alarm. "Look at the time! Wendy and I should be getting back."

Pieter also rose to his feet. "Let me walk a little way with you. Sorry now that I didn't bring the car."

"It's all right, thanks. Wendy and I can walk. Come along, Wendy," and Simonette moved swiftly toward the child playing blissfully in the sand.

"Watch out!" Pieter cried, simultaneously catching hold of Simonette's arm as she stumbled over a stone hidden in the sand. For a long, breathless moment he hung on to her arm in a grip that almost hurt.

A sudden desire to gather her close was strong and demanding, but natural caution reasserted itself and he let her go.

Preoccupied with his own feelings, he did not notice the pulse throbbing wildly in Simonette's throat.

When she and Wendy returned to the house they were met by a frowning Dean, who for the past five minutes had been restlessly pacing up and down the terrace. He was dressed in formal clothes.

"You're late," he observed impatiently, flinging Simonette a sharp scrutiny.

"Only a minute or two by my watch," she murmured breathlessly. "I'm sorry. . . ."

"We met Uncle Pieter on the beach," Wendy piped up. "And Prince, of course. I played in the sand – Auntie Simonette sat talking to Uncle Pieter – "

"Really?" Dean's black brows shot up with something like

distaste. Then, with a shrug, he dismissed the matter as being of no consequence and spoke curtly to Simonette.

"Unfortunately I've had an urgent call to attend a client in Town. I shall be dining with him. I know it's your free evening – "

"That's all right," she hastily assured her employer. "I don't mind staying in tonight." She was anxious to make amends for being late. "Besides, I hadn't planned to go anywhere in particular."

His grateful smile surprised her. "Good! I would have asked Martha to take care of the child, but the poor dear isn't feeling herself this evening and will be turning in directly after you and Wendy have finished dinner. Now I must be off. Goodbye, Miss O'Shea, and thank you."

Simonette entered the kitchen in search of Martha. The old servant sat huddled in her chair, shaking visibly. She gave Simonette a feeble smile.

"Now off you go to bed, Martha! It looks as if you're in for the flu. I'll see to the dinner."

"It's all ready, Missy."

"That's fine. I'll call Wendy and we'll have it here in the kitchen. Now just you leave the washing up to me. Wendy can help wipe the dishes. She's not too young to start learning a few household chores."

This time the old cook-general did not object. Relieved, she ambled outside to her own quarters which adjoined the house.

Later, after seeing her charge safely settled for the night, Simonette retired to her own room and started to prepare for bed. But she did not feel in the least inclined to sleep.

Slipping into a housecoat she wandered out onto the terrace. Though the air was still and warm, gone were the stifling, hot summer nights. A suspicion of an autumn nip was beginning to make itself felt.

How magnificent were the heavens – how vast! Simonette was reminded of the words of the Psalmist, "When I consider thy heavens, the work of thy fingers, the moon and the stars, which thou hast ordained; What is man, that thou art mindful of him. . . ?"

Did God really care? Did He really care what happened to her? Simonette gazed up into the dark blue vault above, as if seeking from it an answer. The crescent moon, the scintillating stars, the lofty mountains silhouetted against the night sky, how grand was God's handiwork! How perfect, how majestic!

Her gaze still riveted on the sky above, Simonette moved in a sort of trance. This time her mind did not revert to the past, to the last few terrifying weeks she'd spent with Robert. Instead her mind did not recede further than that very afternoon.

Just for a brief moment, as Pieter had held her arm, she'd been poignantly aware of a sweet, warm feeling flowing between them. Now she wondered whether she had not imagined it all.

But their conversation had been real enough. With an inward prayer for guidance, Pieter had ventured a question which Simonette had answered in a voice quivering with suppressed emotion.

"You ask whether I still contemplate entering a convent. Most decidedly I intend to take holy vows. Mr. Stanton has engaged me for a year – he has made arrangements to send Wendy to boarding school next year. Naturally I shall fulfill my obligations – I wouldn't dream of letting Dean Stanton down. But at the end of the year I'll be leaving here to become a novice."

"The idea is intolerable." Pieter's low, pained voice was scarcely audible. "You're so lovely, Simonette, so young. You should marry and have children – "

"When Robert died, I gave up all thoughts of marriage. It wouldn't be right, somehow. How can I ever hope to enjoy myself again? How can I ever hope to be happy again?" Her despair, blended with bitterness, tore at Pieter's heart.

"No, a normal life is not for me, I'm afraid."

"What nonsense!" He was deliberately brisk. "That's wrong thinking. Of course you can lead a normal life again. Put the past behind you – refuse to dwell on it any longer. After all, you were not entirely to blame for Robert's death – "

"But I was! Because of me he had that fatal accident. I sent him to his death! I was afraid to marry him, yet afraid to break it off – "

"It's no good to keep on reproaching yourself." Pieter told her. "It's not healthy, you know. You've confessed your sin to God. Trust the Lord to cleanse you from all unrighteousness. Take Him at His Word, 'If we confess our sins, he is faithful and just to forgive us our sins, and to cleanse us from all unrighteousness.' "

Her smile was tremulous. "If only I could believe that!"

Suddenly she remembered Wendy's question – "Have you given your heart to the Lord?"

Was that the same as trusting the Lord to forgive your sins? The priest had given her absolution – but she felt far from forgiven. Her burden of guilt was almost more than she could bear.

Unconsciously she clasped her hands tightly together. It was up to her to make restitution. How else could she hope to atone for her sin except by taking holy vows?

It was the best way possible, her new father confessor had declared. Perhaps the only way, was Father Cunningham's opinion. But Pieter had said. . . .

She must not dwell on what that young man thought or said. What right had he to try to influence her at all? He was an alien to her faith. Besides, he'd not taken holy orders like the priests. What did Pieter know of the tradition of her church or its doctrine? He knew a little, it was true. But how he knew the Scriptures! Pieter had a profound knowledge of the Word of God. Simonette had a sneaking suspicion that he had studied the Bible more diligently, more thoroughly, and searchingly than the priests belonging to her order. All the same, it would be unwise to continue her friendship with Pieter, especially after what had happened this afternoon. Indeed it would be sheer folly. Nothing could ever become of such a friendship. It would be best to nip it in the bud before it had a chance to blossom into something infinitely more precious. Anyway, it was too soon after Robert's death. . . .

With embarrassment Simonette halted in her cogitations. What on earth was she thinking of? What would her father confessor say when she told him her thoughts? Simonette's cheeks flamed with the shame she felt.

Her priest most certainly would condemn her friendship with one who was doing his utmost to turn her from the faith of her late parents; one who was urging her to embrace another religion. Her priest would positively demand that she have no further communication with Pieter Terblanche.

What was it that young man had quoted?

" 'There is one God and one mediator between God and men, the man Christ Jesus.' You'll find that in 1 Tim. 2:5. Why go to Mary or any of the saints when we can go directly to God through Christ? There is not a verse in Scripture to support the doctrine that the dead can intercede for us. We can pray for one another here in this life. And that's what I'm doing for you,

Simonette." Pieter's eyes upon her were tender with longing. "I'm praying that the veil will be lifted from your eyes and that you will be delivered from your supersitition and fear."

Her loyalty to her church asserted itself. "You seem to think my church is powerless to save, that the priests cannot absolve me from my sins." An indignant sparkle flashed from her eyes. Color had crept into her pale cheeks. Her face had suddenly become alive. This was a new Simonette. Her beauty made him hold his breath in wonder and delight.

His determination to win her for the Lord and for himself, if it were God's will, strengthened considerably.

First love was certainly a joyous experience but it could also be most painful, as Pieter was discovering daily. But with God's help he refused to give up hope.

Curbing his natural desire to declare the love that burned so ardently within, he turned his gaze upon the scintillating sea, then to the dog sitting at his feet. Prince looked up hopefully and began to wag his tail in anticipation of a walk.

Resolutely Pieter pulled out a tract from his blazer pocket. "Please, Simonette, won't you read this? It may help you with your problem."

"No." Firmly she shook her head. "Not even to please you, Pieter. I'm sorry. . . . How would you like it if I tried to win you over to my faith?"

"If I were as unhappy, as mixed-up and confused as you, then I'd welcome the effort on your part. It is our Christian duty to help one another."

For a long moment she pondered his statement. "I daresay you're right." She sighed heavily. "I know you mean well, Pieter."

"Thank you. I have not meant any offense. Please believe me."

His sincere tone softened her resolve. "If only I dare – No, not now, Pieter. Some other time I may accept one of your tracts. I tore up the one your sister gave me on the train."

"Which one was that?"

She closed her eyes against the sun, trying to remember the title. "Something about Christ being the solution to our problem. . . ."

"But He is, Simonette! He is. The Lord alone can deliver you. He alone can give you perfect peace. Christ has made the complete sacrifice for sin – there's no need for you to sacrifice yourself. Why won't you accept the salvation God has provided for you? On the Cross He said: 'It is finished!' Wonderful words!" Pieter's eyes glowed gently as he spoke. "The sacrifice of the mass is so unnecessary. I take my authority from the Word of God – not the tradition of the church or of men. Here, let me read what it says in Hebrews chapter 10 verses 11, 12, and 18.

"And every priest standeth daily ministering and offering oftentimes the same sacrifices, which can never take away sins:

"But this man, after he had offered one sacrifice for sins for ever, sat down on the right hand of God. . . .

". . . Now where remission of these is, there is no more offering for sin."

On Sunday morning sitting in her church pew and partaking of the mass, Simonette was strongly reminded of the scripture verses Pieter had read to her from Hebrews chapter ten. If these words were true, then why did the priest daily offer the sacrifice of the mass? God's Word so clearly and definitely stated in verse eighteen – ". . . there is no more offering for sin."

The confusion within her mounted. She could no longer be certain of anything.

After the service she left the church, her thoughts in turmoil and feeling as if she'd been abruptly swept from her anchorage.

Chapter Fourteen

On Sunday afternoon Simonette took a bus ride to Camps Bay. She was too bewildered and distressed, however, to enjoy the beauty of the day or the splendor around her. Peace was everywhere except in her heart, where the storm of confusion and desolation still raged.

But despite her inward tumult, her face was composed, her bearing poised as leisurely she strolled along the beach front.

Suddenly she stopped in her tracks. There was something vaguely familiar about the scenery . . . the narrow main road, modern villas and flats built precariously on the steep cliffs above, the numerous boulders jutting out to meet the sea. This was Clifton, the popular and fashionable seaside resort where the Pearsons lived. Lost in reverie, Simonette had failed to notice that the bus travelled past Clifton en route for Camps Bay. Now she was retracing her journey by foot instead of walking in the opposite direction toward Bakoven.

Just as she spun round a cheerful voice hailed her. "Simonette! How nice to see you. Cliff and I have finished our stroll – now we're on our way home to have tea. You must come and join us." And Pixie Pearson smiled invitingly at Simonette.

She shook her head. "It's very kind of you, Mrs. Pearson – "

"Mrs. Pearson indeed! You must call me Pixie. Now, come along, my dear – "

"But I should be getting back."

"At this time of the afternoon? Nonsense! We haven't seen you since Cliff and I returned from Hermanus. We had a glorious holiday – we have some lovely snapshots to show you. Incidentally, we were thinking of driving down to Sunnycove next weekend, weren't we, Cliff?" Mrs. Pearson flashed her husband an affectionate smile.

"As you say, dear. As you say." With fond amusement he responded to her smile.

"Hasn't it been an absolutely gorgeous day?" Mrs. Pearson chatted on gaily, not giving Simonette a chance to decline the invitation to tea. "Why not sleep over here tonight?"

"Really, Mrs. Pearson, I should be getting back." Decisively Simonette shook her head. "Thanks all the same."

"But you're not on duty until tomorrow morning. What do you say, Cliff?" His wife shot him a significant look.

"Ahem." He paused suitably long enough as if pondering the matter. "I think Miss O'Shea is right, Pixie. If she feels it her duty to return early we mustn't stand in her way."

"Yes, dear – you are so right," Mrs. Pearson concurred, but there was a reluctant tone in her voice.

Their son-in-law had related to them all he'd learned of Simonette's past, that she'd lost her fiancé in a car accident and that she was still grieving for him.

"Poor girl!" Pixie had expressed her sympathy to Dean and her husband. "No wonder Simonette looks so tragic. But she needn't have been quite so evasive about herself. However, we must do all we can to comfort her. Isn't that so, Cliff?"

"As you say, dear – so we must." Though outwardly seeming to approve, Cliff Pearson had certain reservations. He was quite convinced there was more to this car accident than appeared on the surface, else why all the secrecy?

The girl had a haunted expression in her eyes – it was a most unhealthy look. Mr. Pearson viewed with suspicion anything that savored of the neurotic. Though he himself had a secretive streak in his nature, he preferred his fellow men to be frank and above-board. That was why Leila Terblanche appealed to him greatly. There was certainly nothing furtive about that young woman. Candid, gay, carefree, she was at the same time compassionate and understanding and Dean definitely needed a woman to understand him. This Simonette O'Shea, however beautiful she was, would make a most unsuitable partner for their son-in-law.

However, Mr. Pearson was too much of a diplomat to oppose outright his wife's match-making schemes.

"We'll have tea now." He spoke on a decisive note. "Afterwards we'll drive Miss O'Shea to Cape Town station to catch her train."

"Very well, dear. You know best." But Pixie sounded far

from convinced. With a resigned shrug she went into the kitchen to prepare tea.

Immediately Simonette rose and followed her hostess, feeling somehow that she had disappointed her in not consenting to remain overnight.

Later, as Simonette drove with the Pearsons to the station, Pixie observed in a warning voice: "Now, my dear, you mustn't allow Dean to take advantage of you. He's the sort of man who will appreciate a woman more if she's firm with him. Cliff, what are you smiling at?"

"Why nothing, my dear." Hastily he composed himself.

"When you get back," Pixie again turned to Simonette, "you tell Dean that you want to attend your church this evening."

"But I was at mass this morning. I don't usually attend twice on a Sunday."

"Neither do we," Mrs. Pearson seemed glad to announce. "We usually go in the evening, though. On Sunday mornings we like to sleep late. We always enjoy our Saturday nights, don't we, Cliff? We couldn't possibly give up those in order to attend a Sunday morning service. Could we now, honey?"

"No, my dear." And solemnly he shook his head.

The Pearsons, while believing in God, denied the need of a spiritual rebirth.

"All this emphasis on conversion," Pixie would invariably exclaim when the subject was broached, "it's all so unnecessary. It's all right for drunkards and murderers and evil-doers, I suppose. The text so often quoted: 'All have sinned and come short of the glory of God' – surely that doesn't apply to us?" Pixie's smooth brow puckered in a frown. "What harm have Cliff and I ever done? We lead good, respectable lives. We attend church most Sundays. We try to help others. We give liberally to charities. Besides, we can't all be like the Terblanches. I, personally, have a horror of becoming a religious maniac. And so, I'm sure, has Cliff. Haven't you, my dear?"

"Sure . . . sure. . . . But I can't say I'd call the Terblanches religious maniacs. They seem perfectly normal to me."

"I think Leila goes to extremes. The way she influenced poor Sharlene. . . ." And Mrs. Pearson gestured expressively.

And all to the good, had been Mr. Pearson's opinion at the time. Secretly he deplored the fact that their daughter was weak-willed and easily led. They could only be glad that it was Leila who had befriended her, and not some juvenile delinquent. There were too many of the latter running loose today.

On Simonette's return to Sunnycove, a radiant Wendy met her in the hall.

"Goodie! You're home early." The child clapped her hands in delight. "I couldn't wait for you to get back. Guess what?" Wide-eyed, she gazed up into her companion's face.

"Just let me get out of these shoes, Wendy." And Simonette made for her room, the child trailing behind her.

"Wendy!" Dean's voice came sharply from the lounge. "Now don't pester Miss O'Shea. Come here at once!"

"All right, daddy." To Simonette's amazement, the child responded with meek obedience. "But, Auntie, you will come into the lounge when you've taken your shoes off, won't you?"

"Of course. It won't take me a minute to get into something more comfortable. Now you run along, Wendy."

When Simonette entered the lounge, Dean rose in his seat as if to leave the room. Then, apparently changing his mind, he sat down again, but this time opposite Simonette, who had seated herself next to Wendy.

"If you'd like tea, then I'm afraid you'll have to make it yourself," Dean told Simonette with a grimace. "After supper I sent Martha to bed. She's not feeling up to the mark yet."

"I'll make some tea later, thanks. Incidentally, I met Mr. and Mrs. Pearson at Clifton this afternoon. I had tea with them."

Dean regarded Simonette with his sharp lawyer's scrutiny, noting her pallor and the shadows under her somber gray eyes. He was not to know that remorse for the past, mingled with the shame of having to confess to her priest in the confessional last night of her attraction for one not of her faith, had conspired to keep her awake until the early hours of that morning.

"Oh Auntie!" Wendy piped up impatiently, "Please let me tell you my news!"

"Later, Wendy," her father reproved in a stern voice. "Please allow us to finish our conversation."

"Oh daddy. . . ." The animation left the child's face; her toes stopped their wriggling.

Patting Wendy's hand reassuringly, Simonette went on: "The Pearsons are considering coming down to Sunnycove next week-end. Mrs. Pearson will be phoning you some time during the week."

"Oh! How nice!" Wendy enthused before her father could comment.

This Dean failed to do. Instead he remarked that he'd asked Leila Terblanche to tea on Wednesday afternoon, when he would be at home.

"Leila?" Simonette did not succeed in suppressing her surprise.

"Yes." His gaze gave no clue as to his emotions. "I'd like to have a chat with her about Wendy." Dean directed an eloquent glance at his daughter. "Now you may tell Miss O'Shea what happened to you this morning in Sunday school."

The child smiled happily. "I asked Jesus to come into my heart. Auntie Leila asked me if I'd like to and this time I said 'yes.' I got so tired of daddy scolding me," Wendy confessed with the unconscious candor belonging essentially to the young. "And how could I ask God to help me if I wasn't His child?"

"Sounds logical, don't you agree, Miss O'Shea?"

She nodded mutely. He went on, "I was only a few years older than Wendy when I put my trust in the Lord."

"You?" Simonette's expression portrayed her astonishment.

"You seem surprised. Do I look like such a heathen, then?"

"No – that is, I'm sorry – " she floundered helplessly. "It's just that. . . ."

"Because I don't go to church you imagine that I have never known what it is to believe." His lips twisted bitterly. "I have been sadly disillusioned; only my disillusionment was entirely of my own making, I realize that now."

As the child pattered off in search of her doll, Dean took the opportunity to remark to Simonette, "No doubt you have been informed that Wendy's mother died in giving her birth?"

"Yes, so I have. I'm deeply sorry," Simonette murmured in sympathy, striving in vain to fight off her mounting curiosity. What had prompted her employer to speak to her of his past life? During the few months she'd been in his employ, he had kept their relationship on a purely impersonal basis.

Had his daughter's admission begun to awaken something deep within, something precious he had lost at the time of his wife's death? Leila had hinted that Dean Stanton was a backslider. Could that mean that at one time he had shared the same faith as the Terblanches? Had he, too, been ardently religious? It was difficult to believe that such had been the case. Simonette knew instinctively that whatever tragedy befell the Terblanches they would remain loyal and true to their Lord. Their mother had died. . . .

Suddenly Simonette recollected her own mother's burial service, the familiar words the priest had quoted from the book of Job. "The Lord gave, and the Lord hath taken away; blessed be the name of the Lord."

Dean, too, as he sat watching the play of expression across Simonette's face, recalled these same words. Memories, obstinately buried, erupted to the surface of his mind. Sharlene's death had deeply grieved and bewildered him. Bitterly he had blamed God for snatching his beloved wife away from him. After the funeral he had returned with the Pearsons to their home, utterly desolate and frustrated and feeling that life held no more meaning for him.

Powerless to restrain himself, he had cried out: "Take the child and keep her! I don't want to see her again! You give her a name."

The name "Wendy" had been Pixie's choice. In the face of what had occurred, it seemed incongruous to call the child "Faith," the name he and Sharlene had decided upon.

Yes, Dean sighed within himself, for years he'd shirked his responsibilities.

Now, inexplicably, he knew the deep stirrings of regret for his behavior, for his unforgiving attitude. Deliberately he'd turned his back upon the Lord in his time of trouble and testing: he'd ignored the scriptural injunction not to lean upon his own understanding, but to trust the Lord in all things.

What had prompted him to seek out Leila, to invite her to tea? Had the invitation been made merely to discuss Wendy or was it motivated by a stronger reason? Was it that subconsciously he knew that Leila would be able to help him with his spiritual problems, the same as she'd done so frequently in his earlier days? Leila – with her strong, unshakable faith, her cheerful smile, her deep understanding of people's needs – she was a welcome friend indeed.

As he prepared for bed, some well-remembered words from First Chronicles 28:9 seeped through his mind ". . . if thou seek him, he will be found of thee, but if thou forsake him, he will cast thee off for ever."

Was it, Dean wondered in sudden trepidation, was it too late for him to come back to the Lord?

Chapter Fifteen

THE AFTERNOON LEILA came to tea it was cool and breezy, with fleecy white clouds scudding across the azure sky. In the garden trees and flowers danced to the rhythm of white crested waves, crashing against rocks and boulders on the shore below.

It was too breezy to sit out on the terrace, so at Simonette's suggestion, they sat in the sun porch instead. Wendy was thrilled to have Leila visit them and had difficulty in deciding whether to sit next to her companion or next to their guest. She finally drew her stool alongside Leila's, beaming broadly.

"Hope you are pleased over Wendy's decision, Dean." Leila spoke as casually as she could. She had not seen him on Sunday morning when she had driven Wendy back home after Sunday school. In the afternoon when he'd telephoned inviting her to tea, he had not mentioned his daughter at all, deliberately or otherwise. He had sounded detached, almost indifferent.

During tea conversation was fairly general. Leila couldn't wait for Dean to broach the subject. When it became apparent that he was leaving her to take the initiative, she lost no time in speaking of the matter nearest her heart.

Dean's reply came slowly. "Naturally I am pleased. There has been a marked improvement in Wendy's conduct. Isn't that so, Miss O'Shea?" He looked at her intently.

Simonette nodded. "That is so." She spoke guardedly, not wishing to become drawn into a discussion about religion. The Terblanches and the Stantons were Protestants, "defenders of the faith once delivered to the saints," Pieter had termed it. Yet it was a faith alien to her own, one of which she had to be extremely wary. Her parents had been devout Catholics. To embrace another faith, even to take an interest in one, would be sacrilege.

Leila, swift to sense Simonette's embarrassment, turned to

Wendy. "Why not take Auntie Simonette with you when you put dolly to bed?"

"But it's not dolly's bedtime yet. It's still early."

Simonette ignored the entreaty in the blue eyes. "But dolly's sleepy. Come along, Wendy." Simonette was grateful to Leila for the opportunity to escape.

"Oh, very well." Bravely the child held in her disappointment.

When the two had left the lounge, Leila remarked to Dean that even at school his daughter was becoming less willful and more tractable.

"I'd no idea Wendy was any trouble at school," he murmured, arching his brows.

"Not so much this year. But last year she was most disagreeable. I admit Simonette has influenced Wendy a great deal."

"And what about yourself, Leila?" Dean smiled at her. "My dear, you've been wonderful. I'm glad now I was persuaded to let Wendy attend Sunday school. I should have agreed to it when you first approached me."

Dean rose abruptly. "Let's go to my study. I'd rather we talked in there."

He indicated for Leila to take a seat, while he himself began restlessly to pace the room.

Looking at him, she discerned how tired and agitated he was. The sunken eyes and hollow cheeks made her forget her resolve not to allow her emotions to dominate her mind. An emotional involvement with him could so easily lead to unhappiness, even heartbreak.

Her affection for the young lawyer was now stronger, deeper than when as a student teacher she had first fallen in love with him.

"Sit down, Dean." Leila's calm, compassionate voice made him pause and face her with a smile.

"Do you really want to know why I asked you to come here this afternoon?"

"Wasn't it to discuss Wendy?" Leila's heart was pounding uncomfortably. "To be perfectly candid, I half expected you to call on me to express your disapproval, not to invite me to tea. I didn't think you'd be at all pleased to hear of Wendy's conversion."

"When she told me, I was in two minds about it," he admitted ruefully. "A child of seven – it seemed ludicrous, somehow. And yet I was just ten when I first put my trust in the Lord. Such a step for me was fairly easy, my parents were Christians and they were kind, good and extremely helpful – not the sort of parent I have been to my daughter."

Leila caught the note of deep compunction in his voice. Was conviction at long last beginning to grip his stubborn heart?

"Not only have I failed to give her the emotional security that every child needs, but more important still, I have neglected her spiritual education. I may have given Wendy every material comfort while at the same time starved her of the things most needful for a happy, contented, well-balanced life."

"You used to be such a bright Christian, Dean," Leila observed, with an inward prayer that she'd be given the right words to speak. Tact, she reminded herself with a grimace, wasn't exactly her strong point!

"I note that was said in the past tense." Dean's cheek muscles tightened perceptibly. "I'd do anything now to revert it to the present tense."

"Would you, Dean? Would you?" Her eyes were shining with hope. "There's every chance for you to become the man you once were."

His lips twisted cynically. "I was younger then, more gullible and impressionable."

"That may be. But if I remember correctly, you were also faithful and enthusiastic in your churchwork." Leila smiled at him with tranquil confidence. "It wouldn't be difficult for you to find your way back to God."

"Impossible!" he ejaculated with force.

She gestured. "You were always a little obstinate and headstrong."

"You mean because I married Sharlene despite opposition from Pixie?" Dean leaned back in his chair, his eyes resting upon Leila in mock amusement.

"Partly." She hesitated, not quite sure how to proceed. "Mrs. Pearson opposed your marriage chiefly because she considered you were too religious."

"Did she now? From what I was led to understand, the Pearsons considered their daughter too young for marriage. Sharlene looked years younger than her age. She acted young, too, she was so immature in many ways. Though nearly twenty Sharlene was emotionally and mentally still a child."

Dean paused and stared unseeingly out of the window. "We should have waited, the Pearsons were right. But, as you've just reminded me, I was stubborn and self-willed."

He rose and once more began to pace the study floor. "Something you mentioned last week gave me a jolt. You hinted that maybe I had acted contrary to God's will in marrying Sharlene. At the time the very idea shocked me. But since then I've been dwelling on what you said. When Sharlene passed away, I was resentful, bitter, rebellious. God became to me a symbol of cruel fate. My faith was not like the hymnist puts it 'an oaken staff' but a shaky reed."

Leila sighed in sympathy for this man who, at the first great tragedy in his life, had blamed God for something for which he himself might well be responsible. A text from Lamentations flew into her mind.

"Wherefore doth a living man complain, a man for the punishment of his sins?"

"What are you thinking about?" Dean demanded suddenly when Leila did not offer a comment.

"A text from Lamentations." And solemnly she quoted Lamentations 3:39.

"Hm. . . ." He pondered the words. "I wish I had your faith, Leila, your strength and your courage. When both your mother and brother were killed in that car crash, not a murmur against the Lord escaped your lips."

"How do you know? Since Sharlene's death we haven't seen much of you. Rarely do you venture near our home any more. Occasionally you meet dad in the train, it is true. I daresay he's spoken to you."

"Correct. Your father's often told me what a wonderful help you were to him at the time."

Leila smiled fondly. "That's the sort of thing dad would say. In our time of trouble we all trusted the Lord and found in Him a refuge. It's so sad that many turn away from Him in their hour of need. He will not turn away in anger as is often the case with us."

"Aren't you forgetting the words of First Chronicles 28:9?" Dean interjected with a frown.

In response to Leila's glance of inquiry, he resumed: "On Sunday evening this text came clearly back to me. It was one I'd frequently quote in my younger days to my unconverted friends. The latter part of the verse reads '. . . if thou forsake him, he will cast thee off for ever.'" A look of deep despair clouded his clear eyes; his shoulders sagged dejectedly.

"But," she expostulated, "you haven't forsaken the Lord utterly. Surely these words apply to those who stubbornly refuse to repent, to those who turn their backs forever on the Lord. I know many a backslider who in deep contrition has sought the Lord for pardon and cleansing. The text also says: ". . . if thou seek him, he will be found of thee. . . .'" Leila smiled confidently at Dean.

He shrugged. "It's too late for me. For seven long years I have stayed away from Him. And they've been miserable years, I can tell you."

"I believe you. Backsliders are rarely happy people. Some of them put on a facade, but to a discerning person it is plain to see they are quite wretched inside."

Leila stood up. "Sorry, Dean, but I shall have to go."

He appeared far from pleased. "Must you?"

"Yes, I'm afraid so. There's Pieter's supper to see to. He's expecting me back. I said I'd be home around five-thirty. It's well past that now. Besides, Pieter needs the car for a meeting tonight. He's joining dad in Town."

Dean's mind worked rapidly. "Let me call on you this evening, that is, if you're not too tired to continue our discussion."

"I'd be delighted." She flashed him a radiant smile. "Please do come."

She hummed gaily as she went about preparing supper. Pieter, hearing his sister sing, came into the kitchen before being called.

"What's going on?" he queried, noting the sparkle in her green eyes, the excited flush on her cheeks.

"Dean. He's calling here after supper." Leila went on to tell her brother of her chat with the young lawyer.

"Do you think Dean is genuinely wanting to come back to the Lord?"

"Definitely." Leila nodded. "I'm quite convinced of it. At the moment he's in a mental and spiritual turmoil. Oh, I do hope I'll be able to help him!" Meditatively she began to set the table.

Pieter smiled encouragingly at his sister. "I'm sure you will." He hesitated. "I say, how was Simonette? Is she all right?"

Leila darted a swift glance at her brother. Their eyes met and Pieter smiled again. But she was quick to detect the strained, anxious look, the sag of the broad shoulders.

"Say, Piet – is anything bothering you?" Her voice was sympathetic, as usual.

"No. Of course not." Unconsciously he passed a baffled hand across his brow.

"Cheer up, Piet! In time everything will work out all right. . . ."

Dean arrived shortly after supper. Pieter helped his sister with the washing up, so as to give Leila a chance to change her frock.

It was a fairly new dress, one Dean had not seen previously. Despite his inner conflict, his eyes lit up with pleasure at the sight of the green-clad figure standing on the veranda. The electric light played upon her glowing red hair; her lips smiled a warm welcome.

"Piet has just left. Sorry you missed him."

"I came to see you, Leila, not your family." Dean followed her into the lounge and sat down.

She beamed happily as, without further ado, he pulled out a well-worn New Testament.

"I see you mean business."

He nodded emphatically and tapped his New Testament. "What a job it was hunting this out! I'd almost forgotten where I'd put it."

Businesslike and to the point, as usual, Dean thumbed over the pages till he came to Second Peter 2:21. He commenced to read aloud, his vibrant tones filling the room:

"For it had been better for them not to have known the way of righteousness, than, after they have known it, to turn from the holy commandment delivered unto them."

Quizzically he glanced up and met Leila's earnest gaze. "Well – do you think this verse applies to me?" There was a hint of derision in his voice.

Her brows creased. She hesitated.

"Well! Let's hear," he demanded with a touch of impatience.

"Yes. . . . In Hebrews 3:12 we are told to 'Take heed, brethren, lest there be in any of you an evil heart of unbelief, in departing from the living God.' You hardened your heart against God when in blind and willful disobedience you deliberately turned from Him."

Leila paused and opened her Bible. "Now let's not discuss the past – that's over and done with. You want to get right with the Lord, isn't that so, Dean?"

He nodded, his expression grave.

"Well then, let's see what it says in Hosea 14:4: 'I will heal their backsliding, I will love them freely. . . .' "

As Leila read aloud, the words struck a responsive note in his heart. The Lord was prepared to heal his backsliding — what a glorious promise!

A dawning hope touched his eyes.

"Remember this, Dean, God still loves you no matter how deeply you may have grieved Him, and He is more than willing to forgive. . . ."

For weeks — no, months — even years, maybe, he'd been fighting an urgent need to get right with God. No longer could he hold out, the struggle against conviction was too great a strain and he could withhold no longer. The Lord had promised to cleanse and pardon and Dean was now determined to take Him at His Word.

As he bowed his head in silent prayer, Leila was seized by an irresistible impulse to lay her head against his shoulder and to assure the man she loved that joy and peace of mind would once more be his.

She praised the Lord for answer to prayer. The heart that for the past seven years had been defiant and proud had now become humble and submissive to His will.

Chapter Sixteen

SATURDAY MORNING LEILA was finishing some ironing when the telephone rang. She hastened to answer it.

It was Dean's voice and the emotions it stirred made speech difficult.

"Leila?"

"Yes. Hullo, Dean." She endeavored to keep her voice calm but failed in the effort.

"How are you? You sound different somehow. I phoned to ask about tonight. How about a little celebration? Just the four of us, you and Pieter, Simonette and I. I managed to persuade her to come along. And what about Pieter? Would he accept an invitation to dine out?"

Leila's heart lurched in disappointment. The way Dean had said, "Simonette and I. . . ."

"Are you there, Leila?"

"Yes, Dean. A splendid idea. . . . I'd love to join you. I'll just ask Piet. He's out in the garage washing the car."

Leila returned a moment later. "Piet will be glad to accept. Where are you thinking of going, Dean?"

"To Hout Bay. Simonette hasn't been there before."

Simonette again! Stop it! Leila gave herself a mental shake. Now that Dean was once more in fellowship with the Lord, it was only natural that he'd want to help Simonette. Since any attempt to ask her to attend a spiritual meeting would only be met with a definite refusal on her part, an invitation to an informal dinner would be a practical way to open the door of friendship with her.

A pity Piet hadn't thought of the same thing, Leila mused, taking from her wardrobe a dress suitable for the occasion. But then, her brother was so cautious, so inexperienced where girls were concerned. He lacked Dean's initiative and drive. Dean wouldn't let the grass grow under his feet the way Piet was doing in regard to Simonette. If Dean wanted a girl, he'd not hesitate to win and woo her, the same as he'd done with Sharlene. . . .

This new Dean both delighted and astonished Simonette. What had caused such a radical change in him? Surely the fact that he'd rededicated himself to the Lord was not in itself sufficient to effect such a startling transformation? The aloof, cynical expression had given place to one of tranquillity and contentment. No longer was he the haughty, detached employer, or the harsh, exacting father.

Simonette marvelled at Dean's changed attitude to his daughter. He was friendly and approachable, and this new relationship, the unusual display of affection on her father's part, filled Wendy with ecstasy.

On Wednesday evening Dean had returned fairly early after his visit with Leila. Simonette was still awake and had heard him hum a joyous tune. She was surprised but still more so when the following morning he'd asked her if she would object to his reading the Bible and having a word of prayer at the breakfast table. Would she care to join Wendy and himself?

Mystified by his strange behavior, she had murmured a reluctant assent. Then, before she had time to reconsider the matter, he'd explained that last night he had come back to the Lord.

"For years I've been a backslider – rebellious and bitter. But, praise the Lord! – He has forgiven the past. Once again I belong to Him. Now it's up to me to make amends, and I'd be failing in my duty as a Christian parent if I neglected to have daily devotions with my child."

He then opened his Bible and read from Ephesians 2:8. Against her will Simonette found herself listening to the words. "For by grace are ye saved through faith; and that not of yourselves: it is the gift of God: Not of works, lest any man should boast."

Somehow the words stuck and repeated themselves again and again in her mind.

What had impelled her to accept Dean's invitation for this evening? She would be missing her weekly visit to the confessional and that meant trouble. She might even have a personal visit from her new father confessor. At the unwelcome thought, Simonette recoiled in panic.

Successfully stifling her anxious trepidations, she slipped into a rose-colored frock which lent a glow to her pale cheeks and set off her shiny dark hair.

Dean did not comment upon her attractive appearance. Pieter, however, let his gaze linger upon her, and catching his frankly admiring glance, Simonette was aware of a warm tingle of pleasure.

Leila had chosen to dress herself in navy blue, an unusually somber color for her. But the color matched her mood, and Dean, smiling a cheerful greeting, wondered at her pensive expression.

Soon they were driving over Constantia Nek with Dean expertly guiding the sedan down the long, winding avenue leading to Hout Bay.

"What a gorgeous sight!" exclaimed Simonette in spontaneous appreciation.

As they had a few minutes to spare, Dean had driven to the beach and parked the car facing the sea. The sun had already set, but the sky above was brilliant with colors of pink and gold, blue and orange.

With a smile Dean turned to the girl at his side. "I'm quite sure you haven't seen anything like this in Johannesburg, Simonette."

It was the first time he'd addressed her other than Miss O'Shea. Brother and sister felt rather than saw the girl's flush of pleasure.

"No, never! It's too lovely to describe. Is that what is known as the sentinel?" she inquired, nodding in the direction of the long, narrow mountain peak reaching high into the sky.

"It is." Suddenly Dean swung round and surveyed the two occupants in the back seat.

Quizzically he arched his brows. "Why so silent?"

Brother and sister smiled sheepishly. Then Leila's sense of humor asserted itself and she gave a merry chuckle.

"Piet and I are both being slightly ridiculous, isn't that so, Piet?" Hastily she nudged him.

"I guess so," and he grinned boyishly.

"I don't follow." Dean's brow was still raised in question, while a baffled frown furrowed Simonette's forehead.

"Our thoughts were on something else. Sorry," Leila apologized with a flippant air she was far from feeling. "We'll be with you from now on. You lead the way, Dean. We'd better get a move on to the hotel if we want any dinner. And I'm starving. I'll do full justice to the meal, I can assure you. I purposely refrained from eating with my tea this afternoon."

Pieter thrust his sister a grateful glance. Trust Leila to view the situation in its true perspective. It was absurd to feel even a twinge of jealousy at Dean's blossoming friendship with Wendy's companion. Rather he and Leila should rejoice that Dean was now seeking to lead Simonette to Him who alone was "the way, the truth and the life."

Was it, Pieter wondered, the Lord's will for Dean and Simonette to find happiness together? If so, he would just have to accept the fact without doubt, not questioning the Lord's goodness, though it would mean heartache for Leila and himself.

The rest of the evening passed pleasantly. The dinner was delicious and all, except Pieter, did full justice to the excellently prepared meal.

Afterwards, Dean suggested a stroll along the fishing harbor, which was situated on the opposite side of the bay. Though the air was cool, there was no wind and the midnight blue sky above was clear and sparkled with myriads of stars. The sea silently shimmered in the bright moonlight. Automatically Dean fell into step beside Leila, while Pieter was thrilled to have Simonette's company.

She seemed in a happier frame of mind, he saw with relief. Her face had lost some of its pallor and her somber eyes had a strange luster in them.

"You seem different tonight, Simonette."

"Do I? I'm glad you think so."

"I do." His gaze rested lingeringly on her face. "You seem more at peace with yourself."

"You're right. Just for tonight I was determined not to allow the past to spoil my enjoyment of the evening."

"That's the spirit," Pieter approved heartily. "But don't let it be only for tonight, Simonette. Let it be for always."

A frown knitted her brow. "I shall never be truly happy again until I know for sure whether Robert's death was an accident." Always the same question stared her in the face, tormenting her, tantalizing her. "In any case, I was responsible." Her voice quivered with anguish. "In his disturbed mental state I should not have sent him away. . . ."

"You were equally distressed," Pieter reminded her gently. "Don't reproach yourself any more, Simonette. The Lord tells us to cast all our care upon Him, for He cares for us."

The warm pressure of Pieter's hand on hers was comforting and reassuring, as were the words of Scripture.

"I wish you'd confide in Leila," he urged, his voice low. "Of course I've explained to her and Dean that your fiancé was killed in a car crash. That's all I mentioned. I wish you'd tell Leila the rest."

"Oh, I couldn't, not yet, anyway. You're the only one who knows the full story, Pieter. I must confess it was a relief to speak to someone like you."

"I'm deeply honored." He sounded sincere. "I daresay one of these days you'll be confiding in Dean now that he's a changed man."

"Why should I? I don't feel in the least inclined to tell my troubles to Dean Stanton."

"But you will, Simonette, you will. Dean has a forceful way about him. Besides, he'll want to do all he can to help you."

"You are all so kind," was her grateful murmur.

Silence reigned. Pieter could sense that Simonette was deeply moved.

Without speaking they followed Dean and Leila to the car. Opening the door, Dean gestured to Leila to take her seat in the front. Simonette had no option but to climb into the back. As Pieter sat down beside her, her heart began to palpitate in a most erratic fashion.

Impulsively Pieter leaned toward Simonette. "Next weekend it will be Easter." His voice sounded curiously unsteady. "I understand Dean is planning to take Wendy with him on a short holiday."

"Yes, Mr. Stanton did mention something about it," Simonette responded in discreet tones.

"It will be their first holiday together. Previously Dean always went away on his own, while Wendy stayed with her grandparents. Dean hasn't told her yet, but I can well imagine Wendy's excitement and joy when she hears the news."

Simonette smiled fondly. "Wendy will be absolutely thrilled. It will do the child good to be alone with her father for a while."

"But what of you, Simonette?" Pieter put in anxiously. "You'll be all on your own."

"There'll be Martha. . . ."

"Please do come and stay with us – "

"No. I couldn't!"

"Why not? Leila and I would love to have you. You know that, don't you, Simonette?" He spoke with unconcealed tenderness.

"Oh, please don't ask me!" She creased her forehead as if in pain.

"Very well." His tone revealed his acute disappointment.

Silence fell between them, a silence of restraint and inner conflict.

"Enjoying the view, Simonette?" It was Dean's voice addressing her.

She started. Immersed in thought, she'd failed to notice that Dean had taken a different route back to Fish Hoek. They were now driving along Chapman's Peak – a road cut into the mountain and following the coastline for many miles. No artist's brush could adequately portray the rugged grandeur of the panorama before them.

Simonette, who had not seen anything comparable to it in all her life, could only gaze and gaze, her eyes wide with wonderment.

"It's absolutely magnificent," she breathed in awed tones.

"You've said it," Leila declared with emphasis. "We take our scenery here in the Cape for granted. We're so accustomed to being surrounded by beauty that often it escapes our notice. How anyone can continue to be a skeptic after seeing such splendor – " she gestured, "I really wouldn't know."

"I agree there," Simonette rejoined. "How anyone can doubt or deny the existence of a Creator is beyond me."

Pieter nodded in approval and quoted the words of the Psalmist, "The fool hath said in his heart there is no God."

Dean and Leila resumed their conversation. Pieter and Simonette were both silent, as if deliberating deeply.

If only, he mused wryly, he had Dean's self-confidence and charm of manner when it came to conversing with an attractive young woman. He knew well how to handle boys, yes, even young men, yet when it came to dealing with a lovely girl like Simonette, Pieter felt embarrassed and inadequate.

"On Easter Sunday evening," he began awkwardly, "I've been asked to speak at a service in a mission church. I know you usually don't attend your church in the evening, and since you'll be on your own over Easter, it would be wonderful if you'd come along with me." A diffident smile rested on his lips.

"I'd no idea you were a preacher. . . ."

"I'm always glad of an opportunity to speak," he admitted shyly. "How about it, Simonette? Say you'll come."

"Oh, I don't know!" She wrung her hands uncertainly. "I'd like to say yes, honestly I would! But I'd better ask my priest first."

Pieter groaned inwardly. "No, don't do that," was his prompt rejoinder. "You already know the answer to that one."

"Yes, I guess you're right. It's strictly out of bounds to attend a Protestant church service." She hesitated. "All the same I'd like to go."

Joy lit up his eyes. "Do you mean that, Simonette? You'd really come with me even though it means defying your priest?"

She nodded breathlessly, gripped by a curious excitement.

Later that evening, as she sat combing her hair in front of the dressing table mirror, she saw not her own reflection but Pieter's. The revelation startled her so much that she almost dropped her comb. Always the image of Robert was before her, but lately the picture of Pieter, controlled, capable, gentle, was beginning to dominate her mind. Relief blended with joy, only to be swiftly replaced by apprehension and doubt.

What had compelled her to accept his invitation to the mission church? Should she telephone him tomorrow to say she'd changed her mind?

But that, Simonette decided with a grimace at her reflection, would be cowardly. She had given Pieter her promise and she must now be prepared to stand by it.

Chapter Seventeen

THE PEARSONS, THOUGH pleased to hear of the prodigal's return to God, were aggrieved to learn it was Leila who had helped Dean in his spiritual need.

"Dean should have come to us," Pixie complained to her husband. "Now we may as well say good-bye to him for good. He's lost to us forever."

Mr. Pearson pursed his lips reflectively, an odd gleam in his eyes.

"Not necessarily, my dear."

His wife clicked her tongue in vexation. "And here I was hoping that he and Simonette. . . . Now, I suppose, he'll ask that Terblanche woman to marry him and Wendy will grow up to be a religious crank."

"Come, my dear," Cliff consoled his wife. "Look on the bright side. It's not like you to be so pessimistic."

"I know. . . ." She dabbed away an imaginary tear.

"You must admit Dean has changed for the better. See the way he treats Wendy now. What an improvement!"

"But there's no need for Dean to be quite so religious," she protested. "He needn't go to extremes. . . . He was at church this morning when we arrived, and now he says he wants to attend tonight as well. Really!"

Cliff Pearson smiled suavely. "That's Dean all over. He never does things by halves. Intense and purposeful, that's our son-in-law. He means business."

"He'll be our son-in-law no longer. You mark my words, Cliff." Pixie sounded utterly disconsolate.

"Cheer up, dear," He put a comforting arm around her. "There's no need to upset yourself. You have me, darling. I'm here to take care of you." He hugged her close.

"Dearest Cliff," she snuggled against him. "You are so right . . . so right. . . . How would I manage without you?"

Tuesday afternoon when Simonette and Wendy met Mrs. Pearson to select some new clothes for the child, Pixie was her gay self again.

"My word, Dean is getting generous," she exclaimed, upon seeing the check Simonette handed to her from Dean. "All this money for new clothes for Wendy."

"Mr. Stanton would like you to buy yourself a new outfit for Easter, Mrs. Pearson."

"Well, I never!" Pixie's baby blue eyes shone with surprise. "Dean was always so close-fisted. . . ."

Straight after school on Wednesday, Simonette took her young charge to Cape Town to join Dean and the Pearsons for lunch.

"This morning I bought myself a new suit," Pixie told Dean. "Thank you, dear boy. It was kind of you to remember your old mother-in-law."

"Old?" He smiled whimsically. "You'll never grow old, Pixie. You'll always be ageless."

"Dear boy, you do say the most delightful things. . . ."

Lunch was a cheerful occasion. This new Dean, gallant and charming, reminded Simonette of Robert as she first knew him, the Robert who had captivated her so completely.

Now, no more dwelling in the past. Simonette took a firm grip on herself.

On Good Friday morning, sitting in her church pew and partaking of the mass, words of scripture which she had deliberately buried, erupted to the surface of her mind with renewed force, "There is no more offering for sin. . . ."

The fine weather lasted until Saturday morning, when the dark, glowering clouds that had gathered during the night, released their gloomy feelings.

All day on Saturday it rained – hard, sharp strokes beating down in fury. Restless and alone, Simonette stood at the window, watching and thinking. . . .

As she thought of the impending service she'd promised to attend with Pieter, she couldn't altogether repress her thrill of anticipation. Of course, she chided herself, she was being utterly absurd. . . . There could be no future for her and Pieter together. He was of an alien faith. Then there was her shame and guilt of the past. How could she ever dream or hope to enjoy happiness with some other man when, because of her folly and fear, Robert lay cold in his grave?

Within the confines of the convent walls she would have a lifetime in which to expiate the sins of the past. Yes, the convent, she was inclined to agree with her father confessor, was the only place for her. Where else could she find peace?

She woke early on Sunday morning and was relieved to see the sun struggling through the clouds. Everything in the garden looked clean and shiny-bright and her heart filled with a song of praise.

At first the day passed slowly, then, suddenly, it was time to get ready for the evening service. With fingers that were slightly unsteady, she placed a lemon-colored hat on her soft black hair.

Hearing the sound of Pieter's car coming up the driveway, she hurried outside to meet him, a smile of welcome curving her lips.

Climbing out of the car, his hand clasped hers in a "Happy Easter" greeting. His eyes appraised her warmly.

Swiftly she averted her face. She must not, she dared not meet his eyes again. His gently pleading gaze had power to set her pulses pounding.

Meditatively he rested his arms on the steering wheel for a few moments before driving off.

With determination she checked the mounting excitement his presence evoked. She sat silent and subdued while Pieter told her something of the fine spiritual work being done among the colored people by some American missionaries.

"I shouldn't have come, Pieter." With a dubious gesture she turned to him.

"Why not?" He paused. "Once you've attended a service of this kind, you'll want to come again and again, I promise you. You'll enjoy the singing, Simonette. The Cape coloreds, as a rule, have melodious voices, and their radiant faces will warm your heart. You'll never guess that many of these people once led sordid, lawless, immoral lives. Before their conversion, before they accepted Christ as Savior, many of them were drunkards, gamblers, dagga smokers and the like. Now they are living victorious Christian lives – a wonderful witness to the saving power of the Lord Jesus Christ."

Simonette deigned no reply. Everything was so new, so strange to her. Inside the mission church, there were no crucifixes, no pictures of saints. A huge banner bearing the words, "He is Risen!" was suspended across the front of the church which was packed to capacity. Dark shining faces beamed happily in Simonette's direction, making her feel more at ease.

The simplicity of the service impressed her deeply. The singing moved her in a way no singing had ever done before. But what most affected her was the manner in which Pieter delivered his message. He spoke confidently and with convicting power. Enthralled, she listened to the words as they poured forth with such intensity and earnest appeal.

"Jesus said: 'I am the resurrection and the life.' Christ is the Author and Fountain of life. Not the church, but Christ, He alone can save and redeem us. He alone can impart unto us His resurrection life. 'Whosoever liveth and believeth in me shall never die.' That is His promise to us who believe. When by faith we receive Him as our Savior from sin, we are born again to a divine life and this abundant life is found in Christ alone. Through Christ we can directly approach the Father, we can dispense with the intercession of saints. From the scriptures we learn that He is the only Mediator of reconciliation and communion between God and man.

"Because He rose from the dead, we who believe in Him shall also rise to newness of life. Praise God!

"He is no longer on the cross. He is risen! He is gloriously alive. He lives within the heart of every sincere and true believer. . . ."

A mist swam before Simonette's eyes as she joined in the singing of the closing hymn.

"Jesus Christ is risen today. Hallelujah!"

An intense desire to know something of this resurrection life, this new life that was to be found in Christ alone, gripped Simonette with a force that was almost more than she could bear. Only the fear of the priest, the horror and disgrace of excommunication from her church, prevented her from surrendering to the claims of Christ on her life.

Because of the duel going on within her, she bade Pieter a cool, almost curt goodnight. His disappointed look only served to heighten her tension.

For a long time she sat at her dressing table, her chin cupped pensively in her hands. The words "He is risen, He is alive!" reverberated through her mind with an insistence that left her shaken.

Chapter Eighteen

"How was the service?" Leila asked her brother a few days later.

"Fine. The church was packed, as usual. The singing was superb; it couldn't have been better."

"And how did Simonette enjoy the service?"

Pieter rose from his seat and began to pace the kitchen floor, his brow puckered in thought.

"It's difficult to say. She was impressed, yes. With the singing, that is." Pieter paused. "Outwardly Simonette was cool and poised. Yet I could see she was fighting conviction. Tell me, Leila, has Simonette ever spoken to you of her late fiancé?"

"Not a word." Regretfully Leila shook her head. "Is she still grieving for him then?"

Pieter shrugged. "Could be. . . ."

Earnestly Leila looked at her brother. "Piet, won't you tell me what it's all about? It's not just curiosity, you know."

He smiled fondly. "I'd love to confide in you, Leila, honestly I would. But my lips are sealed. I've given Simonette my word. All I can say is that underneath her repose there is conflict. Simonette is a most unhappy girl."

"Don't I know it!" Leila gathered up the tea cups and placed them in the sink.

"Are Dean and Wendy back home yet?" Pieter queried irrelevantly.

His sister nodded. She bent her head over the sink to hide the flush which suddenly suffused her cheeks. She let the water run over the cups before speaking.

"They returned yesterday afternoon. Dean took an extra day off work. Wendy was at school this morning looking the picture of health and happiness. She's put on three pounds in weight, so she tells me."

"So you haven't seen Dean?"

"No. He rang up on Thursday to say goodbye, and asked, well – if we'd keep an eye on Simonette. We've done our best, Piet, but Simonette won't respond. Wonder what's holding her back?"

Pieter sighed audibly.

"What is it?"

"Oh, nothing!" Taking a towel, he commenced to wipe the tea cups.

"I wish you'd tell me what's bothering you, Piet." She was saddened by her brother's appearance. His face was pale and tense, the blue eyes troubled.

"I'm all right, Leila, don't you worry about me." A feeble smile touched his lips.

"You love Simonette, don't you, Piet?"

Mutely he nodded. He was staring unseeingly out of the window.

"Everything will iron itself out in time." Leila smiled encouragingly. "Time is a great healer, Simonette will get over her fiancé's death."

Pieter did not reply immediately. Would the shadow of the past always lie between them? Would Simonette succumb to the fear that was haunting her and be persuaded to enter a convent to atone for her sin?

"It isn't as simple as that, Leila. You don't know the whole setup. If you knew – " He broke off abruptly.

"But the Lord knows." Leila smiled. "Look what's happened to Dean. For years he was a backslider. I could so easily have given up hope. But I just kept on praying, I was quite confident that one day the Lord would answer prayer. So cheer up, Piet."

He considered a moment. "Yes, you're right. It was wrong of me to be so despondent."

"Only the Lord can help us to overcome our depression. Many a time I've been tempted to give up hope. Seeing Dean come back to the Lord was worth the long wait, so let's just go on praying, Piet."

The next few weeks passed slowly for Pieter. On several occasions he telephoned Simonette, inviting her to come out with him, but each time he was met with a firm refusal. Her voice, though polite, held an unmistakable reserve and he was too cautious to try to press her further. He did not want to shy her away from him completely.

As a good Catholic, she was no doubt heeding the injunction to cut all cords with one who was of an alien faith.

One evening, however, seeing Simonette drive alone with Dean along the Fish Hoek road, Pieter could not help conjecturing whether the older man was in some way responsible for Simonette's changed attitude toward himself.

Had Dean with his strong, forceful personality succeeded in winning her affections where he himself had so lamentably failed?

His doubts transmitted themselves to his sister as they lingered over their evening meal. Pieter had scarcely touched his food.

"What's the matter, Piet?" Leila spoke with sisterly concern. She was very fond of her young brother, who though courageous and uncompromising, was also sensitive and cautious.

He shrugged. "Nothing really. . . . Yesterday evening I saw Dean and Simonette drive in the direction of Town."

Leila's brows arched in surprise. After a small silence, she said slowly: "There's nothing odd about that. And yet. . . ." she gestured, "You know, Piet, I had the silly notion that Dean and I could just pick up the threads of our friendship where we left off years ago. But I guess that's right out of the question."

"You mean because of Simonette?" Pieter asked uncertainly, his lips dry.

Leila frowned. "Not really. Dean and I are both older. We've grown apart. That's all there is to it, I guess." Her green eyes were unusually contemplative.

"H'm. . . ." Pieter bit his lip. "Maybe you're right. I had hopes for you and Dean. . . . We haven't seen much of him lately."

"That's true. But we'll be seeing him on Friday. He telephoned earlier today to invite us to join him on a trip to Fransch Hoek."

Pieter took a quick glance at the calendar. "That's the thirty-first – Republic Day. What's made him choose Fransch Hoek, I wonder?"

Leila smiled enigmatically. "I have an idea Dean wants to show Simonette the Huguenot Monument."

"But," Pieter objected, "that will only serve to embarrass the poor girl – "

"Why should it? The Huguenots – the Protestant refugees who emigrated from France are a historic fact."

"All the same, we don't want to cause Simonette any offense."

"Don't worry. Dean will be the soul of discretion. Oh, I do hope it will be a fine day."

The weather was perfect for a winter's day. The air was clear and crisp, the sun shone brightly and the veld was green and fresh after last week's refreshing rains.

Simonette was thrilled with the prospect of a day in the country. So far she had seen so little of the Cape countryside. She was glad it was Dean and not Pieter who had invited her. She was determined to stand by her resolve to have as little to do with him as possible.

However, delight wrestled with disappointment when she learned that Dean's invitation included the Terblanche brother and sister.

Philosophically Simonette accepted their presence, telling herself it was too late to plead an excuse. She would just have to steer clear of Pieter. She must not glance at him – she dared not!

Simonette found the scenery enthralling. Surrounded on three sides by fir-clad hills and mountains, Fransch Hoek, about thirty-five miles from Cape Town, had an old world charm. The town slumbered peacefully in the Drakenstein Valley.

They drove past numerous vineyards and rose nurseries. The Dutch-styled houses were both picturesque and stately.

Wendy gave a squeal of ecstasy as Dean parked the car in view of the Berg River which was in full spate. The river gurgled merrily over the stones as it rushed on its course down the valley.

Holding Wendy's hand, Simonette led her charge to the water's edge. The winter sun, glinting down through interlacing branches of trees, was warm on their faces. Simonette did not look up when they were joined by Pieter, who had an uncomfortable feeling that she was avoiding him.

Conscious of his eyes upon her, she could no longer avert her gaze. She raised her head and shyly smiled at him. With difficulty he repressed a compulsion to fold her in his arms and to declare his love.

"Tell me – " her voice sounded quite breathless, "tell me something about the history of this place."

Successfully he gathered his poise. "Would you really like to know?"

She wondered at his solemn tones. "Yes. I would."

"Just now, on our way to the hotel where we plan to lunch, we'll be passing the Huguenot Monument and Museum. You have heard of the Huguenots, I suppose?"

For a moment she frowned uncomprehendingly. "Vaguely I recollect learning something about them at school. They were refugees from France, were they not?"

"Correct. They were Protestant refugees." He hesitated. "Simonette, if I remember correctly, you told me your mother was French."

She nodded, her eyes downcast. She must not dare to glance at Pieter. His pleading gaze had power to play havoc with her poise.

"Go on, Pieter."

"Very well." He took a deep breath. "The French Protestants, known as the Huguenots, were persecuted by the priesthood for their religious beliefs. When their extermination was ordered, many of the Huguenots came to settle in the Cape, especially here in the Drakenstein Valley."

Pieter paused and smiled placatingly. "Hope I haven't offended you, Simonette."

"No, no. Let's hear the rest."

"Not all the Catholics in France were unsympathetic toward the Huguenots in their struggle against the tyranny of the government. . . ."

Simonette had paled perceptibly. She stood still and silent while Pieter spoke, as if pondering deeply.

"The fugitives arrived here at the Cape sometime between 1688 and 1700. . . ."

"Come on, you two," Leila called gaily. "Have some tea and scones."

Pieter didn't know whether to be relieved or sorry at the interruption.

The Huguenot Memorial, representing religious liberty, was certainly an impressive sight. The statue of a woman mounted on a huge granite globe signified freedom of worship. Glistening above the woman's head was a replica of the sun, being a symbol of the Sun of Righteousness.

Silent and preoccupied, the little party stood for awhile gazing up at the massive structure of the monument and all that it represented.

"Let's go across to the Huguenot Memorial Museum," Leila

suggested presently. "We're supposed to be descendants of the Huguenots. Let's see if our name is on the map." She studied it closely. "Yes, here it is. Terblanche."

Simonette moistened her dry lips. "Somehow I had the idea that your family emigrated from Holland. The way Pieter's name is spelled – "

"Many of the refugees married Dutch settlers."

"Our mother was Scotch," Pieter put in quickly. "Dad is a South African, though, so it's possible that our ancestors hailed from France."

Dean came into view from an adjoining room.

"I've just seen a stinkwood seat which once belonged to Andrew Murray during his residence in Graaff Reinet." Dean beckoned to Simonette. "Come and have a look. Did you know that Andrew Murray's books are still published today?"

Glad to escape from Pieter, Simonette followed Dean. Though outwardly calm and composed, her thoughts were in turmoil.

The rest of the day she purposely kept close to Dean, so close that both Pieter and Leila's belief that there was something between Wendy's father and Simonette was strengthened considerably.

Chapter Nineteen

OLIVIA DE KLERK, DEAN'S secretary, was bored, discouraged and dissatisfied. She was tired of herself and life in general. The change in her employer attracted yet irritated her. Dean's arrogant attitude had given place to one of friendliness. He looked healthier and happier too, not quite so haggard.

With his charming smile and attentive manners, women were once more beginning to notice him and this did not please Olivia. Every attractive lady client was considered a potential rival. Even those whom he conversed with over the telephone, were suspects in Olivia's eyes.

"What's the matter, Olivia?" Her employer spoke with kindly concern. "Lately you've become nervous and jittery. That's not like you."

She smiled inwardly with exultation. So Dean had observed how she was feeling!

"Well, life for me is a bit lonely these days." She eyed Dean morosely.

"Lonely?" He shot her an inquiring glance. "I thought you always had somewhere to go and something to do. Your weekends are usually completely booked up."

"Not this weekend, Dean." Silently her eyes implored him. "You used to take me out sometimes on a Saturday evening. But not any more."

"You know why. I've given up what you consider the gay part of my life, but which was in reality not gay at all. That sort of life can never satisfy."

"You mean," she gestured jerkily, "you now derive pleasure just from attending church and meetings?"

"That's not what I mean." Meditatively he drummed his fingers on the blotting pad on his desk. "Only the Lord can truly satisfy, only the Lord can give inward peace. You need to ask Christ into your life, Olivia. Why don't you? It would make a world of difference to you."

"No thank you." Decisively she shook her head. "But I wouldn't mind attending a service with you some time."

"Well. . . ." he considered a moment. "You say you're free this coming Sunday. Why not take a trip down to Sunnycove and come with me to the morning service at Fish Hoek? Then afterwards you could lunch with us."

It wasn't exactly what Olivia wanted, but it was better than nothing.

Instead of motoring down to Sunnycove, she would take the train and arrive too late for the morning service. In the afternoon she'd suggest to Dean that he drive her back to Town and that she'd be willing to attend an evening service with him. He couldn't very well decline to take her to a Town church. It would mean having tea or supper first in some luxury restaurant or hotel.

In a more cheerful frame of mind, Olivia sat down at her desk and commenced to type the letters her employer had dictated. Life wasn't so bad after all. On Sunday she'd have Dean all to herself; Wendy's companion had the day off on Sundays and usually availed herself of the opportunity to go out for the day. The Pearsons were not likely to be at Sunnycove this weekend, so Dean had told Olivia. There would be no hindrance or embarrassment from that direction.

Olivia's lips pursed in a grim line. Was there any truth in what Mrs. Pearson had hinted, that Dean was interested in Simonette O'Shea? Pixie had positively smirked with triumph when in strict confidence she'd informed Olivia that she believed it was only a matter of time before Simonette became Dean's wife. Her son-in-law was passionately in love with Wendy's beautiful companion.

Well, Olivia grimaced, she'd soon see for herself. Wendy would be sure to know what was going on. She had sharp eyes, that child, in spite of her innocent airs.

Saturday was one of those rare Indian summer days that are sometimes encountered in mid-winter. The air was hot, still and humid. Sunday was not quite so warm. Cool, moist air was coming off the sea from the north, indicating a rapid change in the weather.

Dean had arranged to meet Olivia with the car at Fish Hoek station where the trains were more frequent. She was not on the train scheduled to reach Fish Hoek at ten fifty a.m. With growing impatience he waited for the next one to arrive. Still there was no sign of Olivia. When he hurriedly dialed the number of her flat from a telephone booth, there was no reply.

With a resigned shrug of his slim shoulders, he climbed into his car, heading for the church. He hated being late for a service and somewhat awkwardly seated himself in a back pew.

Meanwhile, Olivia had alighted from the train at Sunnycove station, an exultant smile curving her full red lips. From her carriage window she had spied Dean waiting in vain at Fish Hoek station. Now he would be in church, and apart from the elderly servant there would be no one at home except Dean's little daughter – and that suited Olivia's plans splendidly. She hoped to elicit some valuable information from the child before Dean's return from the morning service.

Wendy was playing with her doll and buggy in the dappled shade on the terrace. Her childish mouth dropped in disappointment when Olivia's sturdy form came into view.

"Thought you were meeting Daddy, that you were going with him to church." There was an accusing note in the childish voice. "He told me so."

"So I was." Olivia feigned a smile. "But I missed my train so came on here instead. Oh, my poor feet!" Olivia kicked off her shoes and collapsed in a cane chair. "That's better. What a long walk from the station."

"Did you come up the steps?" Wendy wanted to know.

Olivia nodded, wiping the perspiration from her brow. "This summer weather, it's no good. We'll all be down with the flu next week."

"Would you like a cool drink?" Wendy asked politely. "I'll go and ask Martha. She's in the kitchen cooking dinner."

"Didn't you go to Sunday school today?"

" 'Course I did!" Wendy nodded emphatically. "I like Sunday school. Auntie Leila brought me home before the church service. Now I'll go and fetch you a cool drink."

"Wait! Don't bother, Wendy. I'm not really thirsty. Come and talk to me, there's a good girl. It's ages since I last saw you."

Recalling the occasion, Wendy giggled merrily.

"What's so amusing?"

Lovingly the child gazed down at her doll in the buggy. "Dolly remembers. She's smiling."

Olivia fumed inwardly. However, not wishing to antagonize Wendy, she assumed a sickly smile.

"Yes, I also remember. But you've apologized, so all is well. Your dolly is very pretty."

Wendy beamed with pride. "You think so? So do I. Yes, she is pretty." Picking up the doll, she hugged her close. "Mummy loves you so very much."

Olivia took the opportunity to enquire: "Wouldn't you also like a mother to look after you? Someone to love you?"

The child gave her a suspicious stare. "I have daddy. He loves me now."

"But wouldn't you like a mother as well?" Olivia persisted. "It would be fun having a mother."

"It depends." Wendy's blue eyes were guarded. "She'd have to be someone special, someone good and kind. Like my Auntie Leila."

"Leila Terblanche!" Olivia was too stunned to control her expression of distaste. "You don't say."

"What's wrong with my Auntie Leila? She is good and kind. She makes lovely cookies and buns. She is pretty, too."

"She's far too fat in my opinion."

"You're horrid! I don't like you at all!" Wendy's voice was raised in disgust.

"Hush, child," Olivia remonstrated with a patience she was far from feeling. "Of course Leila is good and kind. I didn't say she wasn't, did I?"

Wendy pondered a moment. "You didn't say so, but you don't like her."

"Really, Wendy!" Olivia's face wore an air of injured innocence. "How can you say such evil things about me? And you a pupil in Sunday school. You're supposed to think well of people."

The child winced at the reproach in Olivia's voice.

"Sorry, Miss de Klerk." Her apology came slowly. "I think I'll go indoors."

"Come on, Wendy." Olivia was on her feet. "Let's be friends, shall we?" Placatingly she patted the child's golden curls. "You have such lovely hair, my dear."

"I have my mummy's hair, so gran tells me. Did you know my mummy?"

Olivia nodded. "Indeed I did. She was just as sweet to look at as you are."

Mollified the child reached out a hand. "Tell me something about her. Please!"

"Hasn't your father or grannie told you?"

"A little. Mummy was good and sweet. She died when I was a baby."

"Hm. . . . That's only half the truth." A flicker of spite crossed Olivia's face.

"Why do you say that?"

Veiling her expression, Olivia gestured. "Come sit with me and I'll tell you all about it."

"It must be the truth," Wendy insisted, with a dubious glance at her father's secretary.

Olivia flushed with chagrin. "Why, you little – ! Where are your manners, child? Hasn't your father warned you not to be cheeky to your elders?"

Gravely Wendy nodded. "But he has also told me always to speak the truth. And so has Auntie Leila and Simonette."

"Simonette. . . . That's your companion. Do you like her, Wendy?"

"I do!" the child enthused. "Grannie is hoping she'll be my new mummy."

"Did your grannie tell you that, or is it just something you're making up?"

"I'm not making up stories. I know gran would like Simonette to marry my daddy."

"And your father – what does he say?"

"Daddy thinks Simonette is a lovely lady. She is beautiful."

"Beautiful!" Olivia scoffed. "She is skinny and pale-faced. She has hardly a word to say for herself. Anyway, you'll have to say goodbye to your companion when you go to boarding school next year."

"I'm not going to boarding school. Daddy has agreed to let me remain at the Fish Hoek school."

"What?" Olivia bit her lip in vexation. "Well, what do you know?

"Listen, child," she whispered urgently, "you don't really want this Simonette O'Shea to be your new mother, do you?"

Undecided, Wendy shrugged. "Miss O'Shea is real nice. But she's not so jolly as Auntie Leila. Sometimes Simonette is very sad. Daddy thinks it's because she hasn't given her heart to Jesus like we have."

"I wouldn't know about that," Olivia smirked at Wendy. "How would you like to have me for a mother?"

"No thank you," the child's retort came firmly. "I wouldn't want you at all as my mummy."

"Whether you want me or not makes no difference. I'm going to marry your father. Quite soon," Olivia added, covertly watching the child's reaction to her statement.

"That's not true!" Wendy cried in sudden trepidation. The color had drained from her face and she was clenching her small hands in confusion. "I don't believe you. Daddy would never marry you! Never!"

"You're not exactly flattering, are you?" Olivia directed Wendy a baleful glance. "You're a spoiled little brat! You deserve a thoroughly good spanking. When I marry your precious father – "

"I won't let you!" Wendy's eyes were wide with alarm. "I'll run away and hide, that's what I'll do if you dare to marry my daddy."

Olivia snorted with irritation. "Why don't you accept the fact gracefully and let's be friends? I'm quite willing."

Wendy was panting heavily. "I won't let you marry daddy! I won't!" Tears welled up in the blue eyes.

"My dear child, you have no say whatsoever in the matter. So pull yourself together and let's go inside. There's a mist coming up from the sea. By tomorrow we'll have rain," Olivia predicted, pausing suddenly. "By the way, child, I suppose you know what really happened to your mother?"

Her lips quivering, Wendy glared at her father's secretary.

"Your mother died when you were born. Your sweet little mother was afraid of having a baby and that baby was you."

"Mummy wanted me very much," the child countered. "Daddy told me so and I believe him."

"Of course she wanted you – I didn't say anything to the contrary. But she was afraid and so she died. Well – " Olivia stared at the child with unconcealed animosity, "I'm going indoors. It's chilly outside."

Alone, Wendy's tears began to spill over her face. Placing her doll in the buggy, she picked up her cardigan, flung it over her shoulders and made for the steps. Down, down she ran, as fast as her trembling little legs would permit. . . .

Chapter Twenty

"HULLO, OLIVIA," Dean greeted her pleasantly. "Sorry you missed your train."

"So am I." She smiled ruefully. "You did right, of course, in not waiting for me. Maybe you'd like me to come with you to the evening service."

"The evening service?" He looked at his secretary with an abstract air.

Olivia nodded. "Sit down, Dean."

"In a moment. Where's Wendy?"

"Oh, she's outside somewhere." Olivia gestured airily. "I left her playing on the terrace with her doll."

"She wasn't there when I came home. I saw her buggy and doll –"

"Don't worry, Dean. I daresay the child is in her room."

Dean stepped to the lounge doorway. "Wendy," he called, raising his voice. "Daddy's home."

But there was no scampering of feet, no jubilant shout of welcome.

Dean frowned. "That's odd."

"Maybe she's with Martha in the kitchen."

"I'll just go and see. Please excuse me, Olivia."

He was back the next moment, gesturing and creasing his brow in perplexity. "Wendy is nowhere to be seen. Martha thought she was with you. She heard the two of you speaking –"

"We were together on the terrace for awhile," Olivia admitted with some reluctance. "Then I came indoors. It was getting too chilly outside."

"When was this?" Dean looked levelly at his secretary. "I'd like to know the exact time."

"Really, Dean! You're not at the bar cross-examining a witness now. I didn't keep a record of the time – "

"Can't you take a guess?"

"Well, it must have been about ten minutes or so before you came in from church."

He consulted his watch. "That makes twenty minutes in all. Perhaps Wendy has gone to see her friend further down the road. She should be there by now. Just wait while I phone to inquire."

Olivia followed her employer into the study and listened with mixed emotions as he spoke over the phone.

Shaking his head, he replaced the receiver, a suggestion of dismay in the sag of the slim shoulders.

"So your daughter's not at her friend's place," Olivia murmured.

"No." His tone was terse. "Wonder where she's gone? Yes, Martha?" Dean glanced across to where the old servant was hovering in the doorway, a look of horror on her heavy face. "Have you come to ask whether we want any dinner? Do you, Olivia, feel inclined to eat?"

"Well, I must confess I'm rather hungry. I know I could do with something to eat. To starve yourself will hardly help the situation, Dean. You need a little food to fortify you."

He ran undecided fingers through his smooth hair. "First I'll give Leila Terblanche a ring."

"Why not wait until after dinner?" Olivia suggested. "Wendy is not likely to have reached Fish Hoek yet. Besides, Leila is sure to contact you should Wendy arrive at her home. She would know you'd be anxious about your daughter."

Dean scarcely touched his dinner. Olivia, however, ate heartily. She always enjoyed old Martha's cooking and was determined not to allow Wendy's disappearance to spoil her appetite.

Deliberately she lingered over the meal, much to her employer's exasperation.

As soon as Olivia put down her spoon, Dean scraped back his chair and strode into the study. Impatiently he bit his lip as he waited for one of the Terblanches to answer the telephone.

Leila's calm, compassionate voice came over the line. Dean almost cried out, his relief was so intense.

But the next instant relief gave way to consternation. His daughter was not with her beloved Leila.

Appalled, Dean put down the receiver and faced Olivia. His secretary had seated herself on a chair and was sipping her after-dinner coffee with studied composure.

"Wendy's not there." Dean was unable to stem the agitation in his voice. "Leila's coming over at once."

"Coming here?" Olivia sounded ruffled. "What on earth for?"

He flung her a withering look. "How can you ask such a question? Wendy is missing and it's all your fault."

"My fault?" Olivia echoed in scandalized tones. "How dare you accuse me of such a dreadful thing!"

"Sorry, Olivia." Dean was pacing the floor in obvious distress. "Perhaps we should call the police – "

"The police!" Her voice rose in alarm. "No, don't do that, Dean. Wait till Leila comes. Maybe she can suggest something."

Dean hurried out onto the terrace as the sound of a car shattered the uncanny stillness that comes with dense fog. A thick swirling mist was rapidly beginning to blanket the scenery.

"Thank God you've come, Leila! I'm nearly out of my mind with worry."

Her soothing smile had a steadying effect on his taut nerves.

"Try not to worry, Dean. Let's go and find Miss de Klerk. I'd like to question her, if I may. Your secretary could have said something to upset Wendy. That's my guess."

Dean let out a sharp exclamation. "Why didn't I think of that myself? Wendy has never liked Olivia. I daresay the child was provoked into taking flight. She may even have run down the steps; we may find her body huddled somewhere at the bottom – "

His confidence having deserted him, Dean was no longer the cool, collected lawyer. Instead he was a considerably disturbed parent, his mind torn with fear of having lost the child he had just recently begun to love and appreciate. Was this God's punishment for his sinful neglect of his child?

"Come on, Dean!" It was Leila's voice jerking him out of his tortured conjectures. "Will you question Olivia or shall I?"

He ran his fingers through his hair. "Perhaps I'd better."

His secretary was in the lounge pouring herself another cup of coffee. Keenly observing the older girl's trembling hands, Leila was convinced Olivia was in some way responsible for Wendy's disappearance.

"Now then, Olivia," Dean came curtly to the point, "tell me exactly what happened between you and Wendy. I'd like to know what you said to her, word for word."

"I don't know what you mean. Nothing happened as far as I know."

"Now, no hedging." His voice, stern and commanding, sent a shudder of apprehension through Olivia.

"I strongly object to your accusing tone." She summoned all her dignity. "I said nothing to your daughter to which you could possibly take offense."

"Let me be the judge of that. Please repeat your conversation – "

"Look here, Dean," Olivia's dark eyes were blazing with indignation, "things have gone beyond a joke."

"I agree there."

Appealingly Leila turned to Dean's secretary. "This is hardly the time for sparring. We're wasting precious minutes. Can't you please recall something you said to Wendy, some little thing that may have upset her?"

"No, I can't!" With a bang, Olivia put down her coffee cup. She picked up her bag and gloves. "I must be going. I refuse to stay here and be insulted."

"Just a moment." Resolutely Dean placed a detaining hand on his secretary's arm. "You're not leaving here until you tell me exactly what you said to upset Wendy so much."

"Who said she was upset? You're only assuming."

"It's the obvious answer. Out with it, Olivia!" Dean's gaze compelled her to meet his eyes. "If you persist in refusing to tell me the truth, I shall be forced to call in the police."

"You wouldn't dare. Oh, all right! You win. I told your precious daughter that I'd soon be her new mother. Apparently she didn't care for the idea. Well – " Olivia paused dramatically, "I wouldn't marry you, Dean Stanton, if you were the last man on earth. Hope you find in Simonette O'Shea the sort of mother you want for Wendy. My notice will be on your desk first thing tomorrow morning. Goodbye!"

In stricken silence Dean and Leila stared at Olivia's retreating figure.

With an apologetic gesture he turned to Leila. "Sorry that you should have witnessed such an unpleasant scene."

"Don't let that disturb you, Dean." She commanded herself to speak naturally. "Let's – let's go down the steps, shall we? There's no time to lose. Dad and Piet have gone to Town, otherwise I'd have asked them to help in the search."

Dean's cold hand reached out to Leila's, feeling its warmth with a flood of affection.

She let him hold her hand as side by side they gingerly began to descend the steps. The damp, icy mist swirled around them. Their footsteps echoed in the eerie stillness.

When they reached the last step both realized they were trembling. A loud, relieved sigh escaped Dean's lips.

"At least there's no child lying here hurt and helpless, thank God. Wendy must have been desperate to disobey me. She knew she was forbidden to go down the steps alone. She must have been driven to it." Dean paused. "Where do you suggest we go from here?"

"Let's first try the catwalk. Wendy was very fond of running along there." Leila's voice was an unsteady whisper. "She may have hidden behind one of the benches."

"If only this mist would lift! I can scarcely see a step in front of me."

"Let's pray," Leila murmured. "We haven't asked the Lord to help us, you know."

"I've been praying silently. . . ."

"So have I," she confessed, a catch in her voice. "But let's stop and pray aloud. Perhaps Wendy will hear us."

Raising his voice, Dean called his daughter's name. But there was no echoing response, only a weird silence greeted them. Even the sea had ceased its restless tossing.

Unconsciously Dean's hand gripped Leila's, as in prayer he poured out his heart to God.

"Feeling better?"

"Yes, but I can't help wondering – " Dean broke off in confusion.

"What's the matter?"

"Do – do you think this is God's way of punishing me for my spiritual neglect of my child? If anything should happen to Wendy, I'd never forgive myself – "

"Nonsense, Dean! The Lord readily forgave you when, in humble repentance, you came back to Him. Now let's get a move on. And don't despair, Dean. We'll find Wendy. I know the Lord will direct us to her. Look! The mist is already lifting."

"Thank God!" Dean muttered fervently.

Chapter Twenty-one

HALF AN HOUR LATER they almost stumbled over the child. Exhausted by the emotional storm that had loosed her from her moorings, Wendy was fast asleep beside a huge boulder. Her cardigan partly covered her small body.

With a cry of mingled relief and gratitude, her father gathered Wendy in his arms and held her close. She stirred uneasily, muttering in her sleep. "I won't let you. . . . It's not true. Mummy! Mummy!"

Blankly Leila and Dean stared at each other.

"What on earth. . . ." he began.

"Wendy's cold. Let's get her back to the house at once. Can you manage to carry her up the steps, or shall I run up for the car?"

"I can manage fine. Wendy's not a heavyweight."

"Let me carry her till we reach the steps. You'll need all your strength for the big climb."

Dear Leila! Dean murmured to himself. Always so calm, so considerate and compassionate, yet at the same time warm, vital and vigorous.

"What on earth would I do without you?" Unconsciously the words slipped out.

Leila pretended not to hear. She took off her coat and carefully draped it around the cold, shivering form.

"Now let me carry her, Dean," she spoke authoritatively as he nearly tripped over a stone.

"All right then." Smiling ruefully, he handed the child over to Leila. "I guess I'm a little out of form."

"It's the strain. You'll be fine after a short break."

When they reached the steps, she turned to the man at her side. "Here you are, Dean, you can carry Wendy now. Take it slowly while I go on ahead and prepare some hot water bottles. Wendy will need them. Perhaps I should phone the doctor just to give her a check over."

For the rest of the afternoon Leila sat reading in Wendy's room, patiently waiting for the child to awaken. Dean was resting in his study, but she had promised to call him immediately when his daughter awoke.

Toward six o'clock Wendy stirred, then her blue eyes flicked open to stare vacantly into space. Recognition leaped into them when she saw Leila bending over her in tender concern.

"All right, dear? Had a good sleep?"

"Auntie Leila!" Wendy held out her chubby arms. Leila hugged her close.

"Let me go and fetch your daddy. . . ."

"No!" The child's voice rose shrilly. "Let me speak to you first. I remember everything now. That Olivia de Klerk! Oh, she was horrid! She said such dreadful things . . . tell me they're not true!"

"Now don't excite yourself darling. Wouldn't you like something to eat? I'm sure you must be hungry – "

"She said – Miss de Klerk said," Wendy obstinately continued, "that Mummy was afraid to have me – that's why she died – "

"What nonsense!" Leila refuted the words with scorn. Inwardly she was shocked. "Wendy dear, your mother gave her life for you. She wanted you so much, but she wasn't strong, so God thought it best to take her. Your mother is happy with the Lord now. . . . It's natural you should miss not having a mother, but you must be glad you have daddy. Now try and forget what Miss de Klerk said. I assure you she is mistaken. I know she is."

"Oh." Wendy's head fell back onto the pillows. Contentment and complete trust were mirrored in her eyes.

"That's good. But Miss de Klerk also said – "

"What else did she say, Wendy?" Leila spun around in surprise as Dean spoke quietly from the doorway.

"That – that you and she – that she'd be my new mummy. Oh, please don't let her, daddy!"

"You won't see Miss de Klerk again, I promise you, Wendy. Auntie Leila is going to be your new mummy. Aren't you, Leila?"

She stifled her gasp of amazement. She gazed across at

Dean, whose eyes were flashing her a secret message, a message of love and devotion.

She came to a swift decision. Instantly she knew it was the right one.

"I'll be delighted to be your new mummy. I'll stay close to you always, Wendy; so you will never need to be afraid again."

Overwhelmed by emotion, Leila buried her face in the child's golden curls. . . .

Of course her father and brother were pleasantly surprised, as Leila knew they would be when they heard the joyous news.

"But what will happen to Simonette when you marry?" Pieter wanted to know.

"We haven't fixed a date for the wedding yet. There were so many things to discuss."

Leila paused, her lips curving in a secret smile. The way Dean had kissed her! It surpassed anything she had ever dreamed of.

"Dean has engaged Simonette to look after Wendy until the end of the year. No doubt we'll marry in the school vacation. Perhaps just after Christmas. Then we can take Wendy with us on our honeymoon."

"Well, I'm relieved it's you, Leila, and not Simonette Dean wants to marry. And here I was thinking. . . ." Pieter gestured.

"Same here," his sister admitted ruefully. "I asked Dean straight out and he assured me he has no romantic interest whatsoever in Simonette. But I'm not at all sure of her feelings. Could be she cares for him. . . . I'd hate to be the one to dash her hopes. . . ."

The next day Simonette was shocked to learn what had transpired in her absence. "But," Wendy added gleefully, "daddy says it all turned out well. He is going to marry Auntie Leila and I shall have a new mummy. Isn't it marvelous?" Exuberantly Wendy clapped her hands. "Some day I may even have a little sister. I can't wait!"

"That will be lovely, Wendy."

"You don't mind Daddy marrying Auntie Leila?" The child's question held an anxious note.

"Not at all. I'm so pleased. It's the best thing possible. . . . You see, Wendy, I've decided to become a nun. So I'll no longer be able to take care of you."

"A nun!" Wendy echoed, her blue eyes wide with concern. "Oh no, you mustn't. You'll be even sadder than you are now."

"Who said I'm sad?"

"You look sad," Wendy declared with childlike candor. "Even when you smile you are sad. Daddy thinks it's because you don't belong to the Lord. If you give your heart to Him, you'll be really happy. Why don't you, Auntie Simonette?"

A flush of annoyance mounted her face, but before she could reply, Wendy exclaimed: "Oh, here's Auntie Leila! She's come to visit us."

"Feeling better, dear?" Affectionately Leila kissed Wendy. "Your father thought it wise that you give school a break today, especially since it was raining this morning."

"But the sun is shining now. It's lovely out on the terrace," Simonette spoke a little breathlessly. "Congratulations, Leila! I hope you and Dean will be very happy."

"Auntie Simonette is going to be a nun," Wendy chimed in, her gaze filled with regret. "Won't that be sad?"

"A nun!" Leila gasped, her calmness deserting her. Appalled, she stared at the younger girl. "You can't mean it, Simonette."

"Most definitely I do."

"But why? Is it a sudden decision?"

"Not really. I've been considering the matter for some time. Now I'm more determined than ever to enter a convent — to take holy vows."

"Look, Simonette, let's go inside and talk."

"Nothing you may say will alter my decision. My mind is quite made up. Please, I'd rather not discuss it."

"Very well, if that's how you feel. But just tell me this: has it anything to do with Dean?"

"Why should it? I don't follow." Simonette shifted uncertainly in her seat.

"Perhaps I should express myself more clearly." Leila clasped her hands together. "Has — has your decision to become a nun — has it anything to do with Dean and me getting married?"

Involuntarily a smile touched Simonette's lips. "But how ridiculous! I don't care for Dean Stanton at all, well, not in that way. I must confess I like him better now that he has come back to the Lord. He's become more human and approachable. Before I was somewhat afraid of him — he was so austere and aloof. But now I like him since he is different."

Leila's smile was eloquent with relief. "I'm glad to hear it."

She hesitated. "You've admitted what a difference being in fellowship with the Lord has made to Dean. Don't you see, Simonette, accepting the Lord can make a vast difference to your life as well? Becoming a nun can't give you true joy and peace. That's what you're longing for, isn't it? You want peace of mind more than anything else. Complete satisfaction and inner poise can be found only in Christ, not behind high convent walls."

"I wish you wouldn't try to dissuade me, Leila. . . ."

"You're still grieving over your fiancé's death. Is that why?"

"Please don't try to probe me!" Simonette's dark, grave eyes held an indignant sparkle. "I don't like it." She paused. "So you know that my fiancé was killed. What else did your brother tell you?"

"Piet refused to divulge your confidence. So you can rest assured it is safe with him." Rising to her feet, Leila placed a pleading hand on the younger girl's shoulder. "You know what this will mean to Piet, don't you? He'll be absolutely heartbroken. He loves you deeply, Simonette."

Her eyes darkened with the intensity of her feelings. "Go away! Please leave me alone! I can't bear it." Her voice shook with anguish. Cupping her head in her hands, she broke into a fit of smothered weeping.

Leila knelt down beside the forlorn girl and wept with her.

Simonette was so overcome by the other's reaction that her tears stopped suddenly. Dabbing her eyes, she raised her head and whispered apologetically, "Please don't be unhappy for my sake, Leila."

"It's only natural. I've grown quite fond of you, Simonette." A smile wavered on Leila's lips. "You don't really want to be a nun, do you?"

"I – no, not really. . . ." There was agony in Simonette's eyes.

"Please won't you tell me what's troubling you? Perhaps I can help – "

"No one can help!" She flung out her hands in despair. "The convent is the only answer."

"Christ can help. Why won't you give Him a chance, Simonette? Don't close your heart to Him."

She wrinkled her brow, pondering the words. "Can He really? Oh, if only I could believe you!"

"Surely Pieter must have spoken to you?"

"Oh yes, he has, several times. It was an effort not to let

him influence me. It's so easy to mistake emotion for – " Confused, she broke off.

Leila pretended not to notice the younger girl's heightened color. "What is the trouble, Simonette?"

The younger girl stirred uneasily in her seat. "Perhaps I'd better tell you the whole story. It's not exactly pleasant to hear, I'm afraid."

Leila sat back in her chair and listened intently. As Simonette had said, it was not a pleasant story. Leila recognized Robert's threats for what they were – emotional blackmail. Poor girl! she clicked her tongue in sympathy. What a dreadful time Simonette must have had with him.

"No one can blame you for what happened to Robert – "

"But don't you see, Leila? I'm to blame. Indirectly I'm responsible for Robert's death. How do I know it wasn't an accident?"

Always the same question stared her in the face, challenging her, provoking her, never settled.

"Even if it were an accident, I'm still responsible. No matter which way you look at it, I'm to blame." Simonette gave an agonized moan.

"Listen, my dear," said Leila sensibly, "whether you're to blame or not doesn't really matter now. That's all in the past. To atone for your sin, there's no need for you to sacrifice your life. Christ has done it all. He died on the Cross for your sin and mine. In Isaiah 53 we read that the Lord has borne our griefs and carried our sorrows. If you accept His pardon, and His salvation, you will find true peace of mind." Leila's calm, cheerful voice carried conviction. "To take to hiding in a convent is not the answer."

"Then what do you suggest I do?" Simonette wrung her hands. "Oh dear! My father confessor will be most annoyed to hear that I've sought counsel of one who is a heretic."

Leila smiled. "You don't really believe that Dean, Piet and I are heretics, do you?"

"No." Simonette returned her smile. "At first I did – but not now. I believe you are true followers of Christ. I – I'd like to become one, too." Shyly Simonette's hand stole into the older girl's. "Please pray for me, Leila. I'm willing, I'm quite ready now to commit my life to Christ."

"Thank you, dear." Leila's voice was husky with relief and joy. "You won't regret your decision, I promise you."

Chapter Twenty-Two

"SIMONETTE! I CAN SCARCELY believe it." Pieter's voice, filled with awe, came over the telephone. "It's too wonderful. When may I see you? Tonight?"

"No, not tonight," she objected, though not sounding in the least offended. "I'm tired, Pieter. If you don't mind I'd like to get to bed early."

"Tomorrow afternoon then?"

"I'm off Wednesday afternoon and evening. . . ."

"Good! Though it's a pity to wait till then," he said regretfully.

"I'd rather we did. There are so many things I have to consider."

"I understand, Simonette. Sorry for trying to rush you. I'll call for you straight after school and bring you home for supper. Afterwards we can perhaps go to a meeting. Will that suit you?"

"Fine. Thanks, Pieter."

Simonette replaced the receiver, her face animated with gladness. She had no idea belonging to Christ could make such a profound difference in her life. Gone were her fears, her doubts, her frustrations and despair. Instead of chaos, there was calm contentment; instead of sorrow, there was joy.

Leila had prepared an excellent dinner. Afterward Simonette offered to wash the dishes. Leila gratefully accepted her help.

"I promised Wendy I'd be over this evening to put her to bed and to read to her," Leila explained, coming into the kitchen to say goodbye before driving off to Sunnycove.

"Thanks for the lovely meal, Leila." Simonette's eyes shone with gratitude. "You know, I've just thought of something. Why don't you and Dean get married in the September vacation? There's still time for you to hand in your resignation at the school."

"It's an idea." The older girl stroked her hair reflectively. "But what of you, Simonette? What will you do?"

She smiled. "I have made my plans. I'll tell you about them some other time." She stopped short as Pieter came into view.

"Here, let me help with the drying-up. I've just been scanning through the paper. I see there's an evangelistic meeting advertised for this evening in a local church. Care to come, Simonette?"

She nodded. "Please. I've not yet attended such a meeting."

At first she felt strange. Most of the congregation were singing choruses with smiling faces as they waited for the service to commence.

Simonette thrilled again to the opening hymn and joined in with equal fervor. She remembered hearing it sung at the first service she had attended with Pieter. Now she could gladly echo with the hymnwriter, Charles Wesley:

And can it be that I should gain
An interest in the Saviour's blood?
Died He for me, who caused His pain?
For me, who Him to death pursued?
Amazing love! How can it be
That Thou, my God, shouldst die for me!

Long my imprisoned spirit lay
Fast bound in sin and nature's night;
Thine eye diffused a quickening ray –
I woke, the dungeon flamed with light;
My chains fell off, my heart was free
I rose, went forth, and followed Thee.

The evangelist quoted his text from Matthew 11:28 – "Come unto me, all ye that labour and are heavy laden, and I will give you rest."

As she listened in rapt attention to the message, she was conscious of the Lord's presence and power in a way she had not previously known. If she had not already committed her life to Christ, she'd have accompanied the many who responded to the appeal to give their hearts to the Savior.

No longer was she in bondage to the past; she had been ransomed from her sins.

> Out of my bondage, sorrow and night,
> Jesus, I come! Jesus, I come!
> Into Thy freedom, gladness, and light,
> Jesus, I come to Thee!

Simonette praised God afresh for the difference coming to Him had made in her life.

In wonder and admiration Pieter regarded her glowing face, the joyous light in her eyes.

"There's no need for me to ask whether you enjoyed the service. I can see that you did."

"You're right! It was a glorious experience to be present at such a meeting. I'd like to go again and again." She flung back her head and smiled invitingly at him.

"Good!" He responded to her mood of gaiety and relaxation. "You're not tired tonight?"

"Not at all. It's too early to drive back to Sunnycove, unless you're in a hurry. . . ."

He shook his head, hardly daring to gaze at her. "Shall we park here and take a stroll along the catwalk?"

This new Simonette, carefree and vivacious, affected him deeply. She fascinated him in a way the old Simonette had never done. No longer was he able to repress the love which burned so ardently within him. It struggled to the surface, demanding expression.

Shyly his hand stole around hers. The night was calm, cold and cloudless. The moon was high in the sky, the sea sang softly as it lapped against the walk.

In eloquent silence they sauntered on. Then, suddenly, he stopped. Placing his hands on her shoulders, he gazed searchingly into her eyes.

The night did not offer her a cloak, for the moon shone full in her face, clearly revealing the love in her eyes.

"Simonette!" Pieter's lips were on hers. "Darling, I love you so much."

She could not speak for the ecstasy which filled her. For a while she nestled against him; then gently she disengaged herself from his embrace.

She took a deep breath. "I intend to go back to Johannesburg, Pieter."

"To Johannesburg!" He stared at her in dismay. "But why, darling? Why?"

"As soon as Dean and Leila are married, I must return there to try to find out exactly what happened to Robert. I know God has forgiven me – I have no doubts on that point. But I must do all I can to discover what really happened to him. It's most important to me. Don't you see, Pieter dear?"

"Yes, darling, I know." He passed a perplexed hand across his brow. "But it may take months. Couldn't we become engaged before you go?"

She smiled uncertainly. "I may be away some time. It wouldn't be fair, Pieter, to keep you waiting."

Ardently he clasped her hands in his. "I'm prepared to wait indefinitely for you, my darling."

"Oh, Piet!" Simonette's eyes were moist. "I love you, but . . ." she gestured, "I must return to Johannesburg. I dare not marry you with this thing hanging over my head."

"But the past is finished and done with – "

"I know. That's why I can feel happy again. The relief is tremendous."

"Well, Simonette, I won't try to stop you. If you really feel you're doing the right thing. . . ."

"I know I am." She smiled confidently.

Pieter commanded himself to respond to her smile. Then he asked whether she had informed her priest of her intention to leave the Roman Catholic Church.

"Not yet. I have made an appointment to see my priest tomorrow evening. But you're not to worry, Pieter. I shall tell him Christ is my refuge, not the convent. The church can't save, only the Lord can do that." She paused. "Oh, it's glorious to belong to Him!" There was the lilt of rapture in her voice.

Chapter Twenty-three

"THERE, THERE, PIXIE," her husband soothed, stifling a smug smile. "There's no need to cry, you know. No need at all. We must be glad it's not that de Klerk woman Dean is going to marry."

"But I so wanted him to marry Simonette. She's by far the more beautiful of the two. Simonette is cultured and refined, she'd be a great asset to Dean and to us as well. But that Leila – " Mrs. Pearson flung out her hands in disdain. "I can't understand how Dean can find her attractive."

"You forget not all men have the same taste. Leila is a splendid girl. She's mature and sensible. The type of girl who appealed to Dean in his youth need not necessarily appeal to him today. Come on, darling, let me dry your eyes. I like you best when you're smiling. Now give me a kiss and no more tears."

With a contented sigh she leaned against her husband. "What would I do without you, Cliff? You're always so understanding. It could be Leila is the right choice for Dean. If only she weren't so religious!"

"I hear from Dean that Simonette O'Shea has left the Catholic church."

"Has she really? I suppose we should be glad. But it makes no difference now. None at all."

"How about dining out tonight? And put on that new dress you bought yesterday. You look lovely in it, darling."

"Do you think so?" Pixie's blue eyes shone like sapphires.

Cliff Pearson nodded. "Tomorrow afternoon we'll take a trip down to Sunnycove and congratulate Dean in person."

"Oh, Cliff – I couldn't!" Pixie's blue eyes clouded over. "Not just yet."

"But you'll have to get used to the idea of Leila being Wendy's stepmother. And the sooner the better. However, it's some consolation to know we'll always be Wendy's grandparents even though Dean and Leila may have children of their own."

"Surely they won't. It wouldn't be fair to Wendy."

"Nonsense! It will do the child a world of good to have a couple of brothers or sisters. Now no more of this sort of talk. You'd better go and get ready, Pixie. I know you like to take your time when dressing to go out."

"Very well, Cliff. I'll do my best to be pleasant to Leila when we see her tomorrow, even though it goes against the grain. I'm doing it for your sake, Cliff."

"Thank you, my dear. You're very sweet, Pixie. No man could have a more delightful wife."

"Oh, Cliff!" She buried her golden head against his chest.

He smiled with satisfaction. Firmness, tempered with just the right touch of flattery and affection, went a long way toward achieving domestic bliss.

Saturday afternoon passed fairly pleasantly. Genially Cliff Pearson beamed at the happy couple as he shook hands with them. His wife, taking her cue from him, extended a slim, dainty hand to Leila, who clasped the older woman's hand in sincere appreciation.

"And when are you two planning to be married?" Cliff wanted to know, accepting the cup of tea Leila handed to him.

"In the September school holidays," his son-in-law answered. "We had thought of waiting till the end of the year, but now that Simonette is returning to Johannesburg — "

With a startled exclamation Pixie interrupted him. "She's going back! But why, Dean? Is she so heartbroken? Poor girl!"

Dean smiled at his mother-in-law. "Now don't jump to absurd conclusions, Pixie. It's not at all like that, I can assure you. Simonette is genuinely pleased that Leila and I are being married. She's employed till the end of the year, I know. But as she herself so sensibly pointed out, why wait until then, when it will be to our mutual advantage if she left a few months earlier. Leila plans to give up teaching and will stay home to take care of Wendy."

"Quite, quite." Cliff Pearson nodded with approval.

"But why does Simonette wish to return to Johannesburg?" Pixie persisted, inclining her head in Leila's direction.

"It's a personal matter, Mrs. Pearson," Leila replied, "Simonette has her own reasons. We're sorry she's going, of course, deeply sorry."

"Are you sure it's not on account of you and Dean – "

"Quite positive, Mrs. Pearson. I myself thought she cared for Dean," Leila confessed, "but I was mistaken. Very much so." She caught her fiancé's gaze and smiled.

"There's something odd about that girl," Mr. Pearson intervened, directing a shrewd glance at his son-in-law.

"There's nothing strange about Simonette," Leila put in. "Now that we know her true position. . . ."

"Ah! So at last she has decided to confide in you." Mr. Pearson gave Leila an encouraging smile. "It would be a good thing for you to enlighten us, Leila. We don't want to go on misjudging the girl."

Leila glanced at her fiancé before speaking. He nodded in assent.

"As you've already heard from Dean, Simonette has left the Catholic church. She has now given her life to God. She had some idea in her mind about becoming a nun. However, I managed to convince her that Christ alone was the answer to her need. She has proved that for herself now. Only the Lord can satisfy a seeking soul."

Pixie Pearson shifted uncomfortably in her seat. Trust that Terblanche girl to start preaching a sermon. She was on the point of making a caustic rejoinder when her husband spoke.

"Well, as long as the girl is happy again – " Mr. Pearson gestured. "I knew she had something on her mind, poor girl." Deftly he changed the conversation by asking Dean where his ex-secretary was now employed.

"I understand Miss de Klerk is now working for a firm of accountants." Dean spoke casually.

"Rather odd – don't you agree – changing her job so suddenly? What has Miss de Klerk's uncle to say about the matter?"

At the mention of Olivia's name, Wendy was on the alert. "She wanted to be my new mummy," the child piped up. "But I wouldn't let her. She was very nasty about it."

"Oh, you poor dear!" Fondly Mrs. Pearson stroked her grandchild's golden curls.

"I ran away and hid myself." With martyred pride, Wendy

resumed her story, "But Auntie Leila and daddy found me. They were so cross 'cause I ran down the steps — "

Mrs. Pearson gasped in horror. But before she could speak, Wendy continued: "But daddy forgave me for being disobedient. He said we must thank God for taking care of me, that I didn't fall. But I promised never to go down the steps again on my own. Never! So cross my heart." And solemnly the child gazed at her father.

"Wendy could have fallen and injured herself badly." Pixie looked approvingly at her son-in-law. "I hope you have informed Miss de Klerk's uncle of her disgraceful behavior in frightening poor Wendy to take flight."

Dean was silent. Then he slowly observed: "Telling old Mr. de Klerk wouldn't help matters in any way. It would only upset him. No harm has come to Wendy, thank God, and Leila and I, well, we discovered each other that afternoon."

"Ah, so that's how it came about," Mr. Pearson murmured, suppressing a chuckle. "Well, some good did come out of it after all."

"How can you say that, Cliff?" his wife objected. "Wendy could have fallen."

"But she didn't. Now Wendy is to have a new mother. There will be no Olivia de Klerk to bother the child any more — or Dean, for that matter. We must be glad, Pixie, that our son-in-law has chosen so wisely."

Mrs. Pearson smiled sweetly in her husband's direction. "You are so right, Cliff. So right. . . ."

* * *

Olivia de Klerk glanced up in displeasure when on Tuesday morning the junior accountant approached her desk. In no way did Ken Mitchell appeal to her. He lacked Dean's reserve and dignity; he was too free and easy and fancied himself something of a lady's man.

She hated typing balance sheets. She missed the excitement that lurked beneath the air of outward calm that was part of a legal firm, missed meeting interesting people. But most of all she missed Dean's friendship, missed it more than she dared to admit.

But she alone was to blame. It was too late now for regrets.

"Hullo there." Ken Mitchell seated himself on her office desk, quite unruffled.

I like your cool cheek! Somehow Olivia refrained from uttering the sharp retort. She sat with tightly compressed lips.

"How about going out with me tonight?"

Vehemently Olivia shook her head. "No, thanks. If you don't mind getting off my desk – I have work to do. I must finish this balance sheet before lunch."

"My, we are being starchy. You Cape girls aren't half as friendly as your Joburg sisters."

"Hm. . . . So you hail from Johannesburg?"

"Correct."

Olivia's mind worked rapidly. "I don't suppose you knew a girl up there by the name of Simonette O'Shea?"

"Simonette O'Shea!" In his excitement Ken Mitchell jumped off Olivia's desk.

"Why, do you know her?" Olivia cloaked her curiosity with an effort.

"Sure I do. I know her very well."

"Oh." Quickly Olivia schooled her expression. "Please tell me something about her."

"Do you know her then?" he countered.

"In a way," Olivia's response came guardedly.

"Perhaps you could give me Miss O'Shea's address. I'm most anxious to get in touch with her again."

"Tell me, is she in some sort of trouble?"

"Trouble?" His brows shot up. "Not that I know of. Toward the end of last year she had a terrific shock, poor girl. Her fiancé was killed in a car crash."

"Is that all?"

"You sound disappointed, Miss de Klerk. What exactly did you expect to hear?"

"It doesn't matter. . . . Involuntarily Olivia let out a hysterical laugh.

Nothing mattered any more. Her visit to Dean's home had been futile, or rather, it had had unexpected repercussions. Mrs. Pearson's insinuations regarding Dean and Wendy's companion were utterly without foundation, mere wishful thinking on Pixie's part, no doubt.

Now Dean was engaged to marry Leila Terblanche, of all people!

You've been a little idiot, severely Olivia admonished herself. *Through your foolishness you've lost Dean for good.*

Ken Mitchell's voice intruded sharply. "Well, how do I get in touch with Miss O'Shea? Is she in the telephone book?"

Mutely Olivia nodded. Ken began impatiently to thumb through a telephone directory.

"Under what name, please?"

"Dean Stanton of Sunnycove. Miss O'Shea is his daughter's companion. But she won't be that much longer as Mr. Stanton is shortly to be married again. . . ."

But Ken Mitchell was not listening. Purposefully he strode into his own office and lifting the telephone receiver, dialed the Stanton home. A curious smile played on his lips.

Chapter Twenty-four

THE DAY WAS BRIGHT and sunny without a cloud; the air was still and softly scented with early spring flowers.

Simonette was on the point of closing the front door behind her, when the sound of the telephone made her hurry back into the house to answer the ring.

"Hullo!" she spoke a trifle impatiently into the mouthpiece.

"Is that you, Simonette? Ken Mitchell here."

Astonished, she was bereft of speech for a few moments before replying.

"Yes," she rejoined breathlessly, "this is Simonette O'Shea."

"Good! When may I see you again? Some time this afternoon?"

"No. I'm sorry, Ken," she faltered, "I'd rather not see you again."

"But you must! I have something important to tell you."

"I – " She stood undecided, slipping a hand through her carefully combed hair.

"If you don't mind, Ken – "

"Listen, Simonette! You looked ghastly the last time I saw you. Positively tragic. You could have spared yourself a great deal of unnecessary grief, but you ran away when I wanted to speak to you. This time I won't let you escape. It's for your own good, my girl."

She took a deep breath. "I must go now. I'm late as it is. I'm meeting my little charge after school."

"I shall be down to see you after office hours."

"Very well," she promised reluctantly, "I shall be waiting."

As the time drew rapidly near for her to meet Ken, Simonette told herself not to feel nervous. After all, Christ had healed the wounds of the past, so what was there to be afraid of? Did

Ken know something about Robert of which she herself was ignorant? Perhaps he might even know what actually happened to her late fiancé, whether his death was an accident or not.

Why hadn't she thought of that before? Simonette wondered, suddenly anxious to meet Ken again.

But she was quite unprepared for what Ken Mitchell had to tell her.

They had arranged to meet in a restaurant near Fish Hoek beach. As Simonette poured the tea, Ken remarked: "From the way you've been avoiding me, it's fairly obvious you haven't the faintest clue as to what actually caused Robert's death."

Frowning, Simonette stared at Ken. "He was killed in a car accident. You know that as well as I do."

"Ah yes." Ken leaned back in his chair and surveyed her quizzically. "But you've been laboring under the impression that it was your fault, you've been blaming yourself for his death, haven't you?"

"Yes." Slowly Simonette sipped her tea. "But how did you know?"

"We'll skip that part for the time being." He paused, took a gulp of tea, and announced dramatically: "Robert was a drug addict."

"A drug addict!" she ejaculated, caught between remorse and relief. "I just can't believe it. You're not joking?"

"Why should I? It's the truth, I tell you."

"There was an inquest. Why didn't you come forward at the time?" Simonette demanded with a touch of indignation.

"The day before the inquest I was called away urgently on business. When I returned to Johannesburg, it was to find that you were already on the train bound for Cape Town. I came running alongside the platform, remember? I shouted out to you, but you ignored me. Then earlier this year I saw you in a café in Sea Point. Again you refused to let me speak to you. You fled as if your very life was in danger."

Her eyes held a dazed look. "Drugs! I can scarcely believe it even now." She knew a pang of compassion. "Oh no. How horrible! So that's why Robert changed so toward me. . . . Poor Robert! But what on earth started him on such a dangerous habit?"

"Robert lacked self-confidence. He needed something to bolster up his ego. He was incredibly vain. . . ."

"So I was not really to blame," murmured Simonette softly. "What a relief!" Her eyes smarted with repressed tears.

"I warned Robert that he had no business marrying you, that instead he should go away for treatment. But he wouldn't hear of it. From him I learned that you threatened to break off the engagement and that to hold you to your promise, he had threatened suicide. What a deplorable situation for you! It was nothing short of emotional blackmail. But don't judge him too harshly, Simonette. Robert wasn't always responsible for his actions."

"It's not for me to judge him, Ken." Simonette halted, her expression meditative. "What a waste of a life. What an appalling waste! Robert was young and gifted, he would have made his mark in life. Yet a life lived without God is a wasted life."

Ken arched his eyebrows. "Somehow you've changed, Simonette. You've changed a lot since I last saw you."

Simonette nodded. "I can well believe that. I have now committed my life to the Lord. It happened fairly recently, as a matter of fact. I was desperate – absolutely desperate. I felt I had to somehow atone for Robert's death. I was prepared to sacrifice my life and to enter a convent. But praise God, I saw the light just in time. A friend helped me find the Lord. I have left the Catholic church," she added, her inner peace and poise reflected in her tranquil expression.

"Well! You don't say." Ken sounded and looked surprised. "You were such a staunch Catholic, Simonette. Nothing could shake your faith."

"I wouldn't call it faith," she demurred with a smile. "I'd say it was a belief based on fear, superstition, and tradition. But now Christ to me is no longer merely a figure on a cross. He is a living reality. That's the difference."

"Ah, well. . . ." Ken shrugged complacently, "I never did have much time for religion of any kind."

"But if you're ever in need of any spiritual help, you can count on me. My husband-to-be – "

Ken interrupted: "Your husband! But that de Klerk woman said. . . . You mean to say you're to be married to that lawyer Dean Stanton?"

She laughed softly. "No, not to him. But what did Olivia de Klerk say?"

"That you won't be Stanton's daughter's companion much longer. He is shortly to be married again."

"That's correct. Mr. Stanton is engaged to marry my future sister-in-law."

Before returning to Cape Town, Ken Mitchell drove Simonette back to Sunnycove.

"Goodbye for the time being." She held out her hand to him. "And thank you."

Dean was late coming home from the office and Simonette could barely wait for dinner to be over. It was well after eight-thirty before she was finally free for the evening. Wendy had insisted that she read two bedtime stories instead of the usual one.

It's too late now, Simonette decided, to walk over to see Pieter. She would have to telephone him instead.

But the telephone was switched through to Dean's study where he was busy working on an important brief.

Well, that's that! She would have to wait till tomorrow to contact Pieter.

As she crossed the hall, Dean emerged from his study. "Wendy asleep?"

Simonette nodded. Dean went on, "I think I'll just take a run over to Fish Hoek to see Leila. It's such a delightful evening. Any message for Pieter?"

"Well – " Simonette hesitated. She was still somewhat in awe of Dean. "Would it be possible for me to come over with you? Martha's still up – she's busy ironing in the kitchen, so Wendy should be all right. Pieter can bring me back at once."

"Of course, of course." Dean nodded absently.

Brother and sister were both at home. Leila was in the kitchen sewing; Pieter had just finished correcting a pile of exercise books. Both were pleased with the unexpected visit, especially Pieter, who had been earnestly praying that Simonette would not find it necessary to return to Johannesburg.

"I have something important to tell you," she began in a rush before Pieter could speak. "Something so marvelous yet at the same time so tragic."

Three pairs of curious eyes were focused upon her.

"Let's go into the lounge and sit down," Leila suggested, taking Simonette's arm.

All three listened in sober silence while Simonette related